D1524357

MURDER ACROSS THE SHADOWED ROOM

BLYTHE BAKER

When Lillian Crawford's parents sent her to stay with wealthy relatives in England, they hoped she would return a refined lady, having outgrown her headstrong ways. Instead, Lillian and her twin brother Felix stumble headfirst from one adventure into another.

While attending a concert in the city, Lillian witnesses a deadly crime that sets her off on a new investigation to uncover the identity of a killer who will stop at nothing to silence the one woman who stands in his way...

1

_____

"Your bishop? Are you sure about that?"

I looked up from my plate of half-finished fruit, eyeing my twin brother Felix, who sat across from me at the long dining room table. A chess board sat between he and our young second cousin, William, who stared at the marble and onyx squares as if willing them to move with his mind alone.

"Yes," William answered, turning his furrowed face up at my brother. "Why would I not be?"

Felix shrugged, leaning back in his seat. He may have been smirking, but the glint in his eyes was all I needed to see that he had every intention of teaching the boy a lesson or two in the ways of a proper chess game. As soon as Felix had started to play, upon our arrival in the house, it had drawn William's curiosity, and they had begun games that would last sometimes for days.

William's wide blue eyes swept over the board again, examining each of his pieces that remained. Felix had taken four of his pawns, his rook, and both his knights.

Even from where I sat, I could see there were at least three moves that he could make, one of which would keep Felix entirely away from the queen. Stealing the queen was one of Felix's favorite maneuvers.

"William, have you eaten enough?" the question came from his father, Richard, who sat at the head of the table.

I turned to look, and saw Cousin Richard and the several guests he had invited over for luncheon were all looking keenly at the boy.

The luncheon was, in a way, a celebration of William's return to the family. After he had survived a recent kidnapping and been safely rescued, Richard wanted to mark the occasion of his return by throwing several parties. This morning was merely the latest in these jubilations.

"Yes, Father," William said, his eyes not leaving the chessboard.

"Are you certain?" Richard asked. "I don't believe you have been eating well enough since coming back home."

William took a quick glance at his plate, snatched a piece of bacon from the plate, popped it between his teeth, and returned his attention to the game.

"He's doing just fine, Richard," said a gentle voice beside him.

Miss Rosaline, to the surprise of us all, had come to every one of the celebratory get togethers. I had thought for certain she would have written Richard off for briefly accusing her of taking his son the way he had. Instead, though, it seemed the honest conversation they'd had made her, and he, think about the relationship they shared.

"Yes, I imagine the lad is just happy to be home," said

another man to his left, a one Mr. Rogers. "He is doing as he should, distracting himself and putting his mind to productive pursuits. These sorts of endeavors will help him forget his time away from home."

Richard seemed less convinced, but said nothing.

"He is doing just fine," Rosaline repeated, laying a gentle hand on Richard's arm. "You cannot will everything to be as it was."

"I realize that," Richard said, somewhat heavily. "And I am grateful just to have him safe again."

He glanced toward me, and I could see the truth in his gaze.

I gave him a small, proud smile before turning to look back at the game.

In a way, I completely understood what my mother's cousin meant. I could not will things to be as they were... but in a way, I wished I could.

It would certainly make some *things easier to deal with now.*

I glanced at Felix, watching as he studied William's wary hand upon one of his pawns. Outwardly, my brother looked exactly as he always did, his dark hair sleeked back from his forehead, his long-legged frame clad in a grey lounge suit, stylish yet casual enough for the occasion. His brow was smooth, his expression entirely untroubled, with his arm resting on the table, his legs crossed one over the other, bouncing slightly. From the look of him, there was no place else he'd rather be.

Either he concealed his worry very well...or he really was not thinking about the conversation we had just had three days prior, the conversation wherein he told me that the death of our younger brother, Daniel, had not been an accident.

We had not spoken of it again. Had not spoken of *him* again. Not that I wanted to, of course. The morning he'd opened his mouth about it had been after one of no sleep, after several nights of little sleep. I had dismissed it as nothing more than worry about William, and the staggeringly difficult days we had endured. How could he not think of Daniel after William had been kidnapped? William was not much younger than Daniel had been, and the idea of the boy not surviving the ordeal had been...well, too much for either of us to bear, really.

Maybe Felix had just said what he'd said without thinking, his mind not as clear or sharp as it typically was. That was an easy explanation, of course.

The trouble was that *I* could not stop thinking about it now, and whether or not what he'd said had been in jest, self-deprecation, or worst of all, the truth. I could hardly bear the idea that he somehow had been responsible for Daniel's death. It just...didn't make sense.

What did make sense was that he'd blamed himself for the accident all those years before. It had nearly eaten him alive. His cool, indifferent exterior was nothing more than a shield to hide his true thoughts, which were often plagued with anxiety and doubt. But I knew that of him. I knew him better than I knew myself, better than he knew himself.

That was how it was, as his twin. We were closer than ordinary siblings could ever be. He was my right hand, I his left.

Felix glanced at me as if my thoughts had somehow drifted across the table to him, and gave me a lazy stare

before returning his gaze back to the board, where William had decided to finally let go of the pawn.

What, then, was this distance between us? We had never gone so long dancing around something before, something that was so big and so important, yet we both seemed to ignore it when we were around one another? Why?

"Sir, tea will be served out on the terrace," Hughes, the butler, said as he entered the room.

"Very good," Richard said, getting to his feet. "Well, if you all would care to join me outside."

The group rose, one by one, talking of their appreciation for the lovely weather we had been having and the anticipation of tea after such a delicious meal.

"Father, may we finish our game?" William asked.

Richard lingered near the door as the other guests passed by.

The stricken look on his face told me that it would be a long, long while before he could comfortably leave William out of his sight. His jaw muscle tightened, and he tried to force a smile. "Yes, all right," he said. "But don't take too long. You need some fresh air today."

William nodded obediently, but it was clear his mind was filled with the chess game.

"Keep an eye on him, will you?" Richard asked in a lower voice, his eyes falling upon me.

"Of course," I said.

Richard nodded, his gaze lingering on the boy for a moment before forcing himself to turn and walk away.

"You really shouldn't worry your Father so," I said, pushing my finished plate aside, leaning on my arms. "If he had his way, he'd have you glued to his side so that nothing could happen to you."

William looked up at me. "It's not as if you or Felix are going to let anything happen to me," he said.

"We certainly would not," Felix said. "Your father is just very happy to have you home."

"I'm happy to be home, too," William said.

Felix glanced at me in warning, telling me not to say anything further. It seemed that everyone in the household had an unspoken agreement about not telling the boy how much danger he had truly been in.

I looked down at my wrist, which had been wrapped tightly by one of Richard's friends, a physician who knew at a single glance that I'd sprained it when the kidnapper had thrown me during a struggle. It felt better, even after a few days, but I knew I still had to be careful with it.

William had yet to mention the whole ordeal with fleeing the room he had been imprisoned in, but I imagined that if he ever thought of it, it would have frightened him. Now that the danger had passed, it was probably much easier for him not to dwell on it all too much.

The door to the dining room opened once more, and Hughes stepped in again.

"Yes, we know Richard wishes for us to follow him," I said, getting to my feet. "We were not dawdling, just letting the boys finish their game."

"Oh, we're miles away from finishing," Felix said with hardly a look up. "We could be here all afternoon."

William's brow furrowed. "I don't think it will take me that long."

"At the rate you are going right now, we could be here until the end of next week," Felix said.

"It's not that, Miss," Hughes said. "Mr. Eugene Osbourn is here to see you. I assumed you were out with the others, and so, he is outside waiting for you."

"Mr. Osbourn?" I asked, my forehead wrinkling. "What's he doing here?"

Felix got to his feet. "Coming to see you," he said. "Come on, William, we'll pick this up later."

"But I was just about to checkmate you," William said, frowning.

"Of course you were," Felix said, doubtfully. "Let's go see Mr. Osbourn, shall we?"

William was not at all pleased with this idea, but followed us out all the same.

The other guests had made themselves comfortable out on the terrace. The round table was already occupied by Miss Rosaline, Mr. and Mrs. Rogers, and Richard, all of whom were playing cards.

Mr. Osbourn stood beside them, staring out over the garden, engaged in conversation with Richard and the others.

As we approached, he turned to regard us, and smiled.

It struck me, upon seeing him again, how blue his eyes were. For some reason, I still half expected to see him wearing the dark shades that he'd worn when we had first met, as he had been so recently cured of his blindness. He stood straight and tall, dressed in a fine suit, a grey fedora tucked beneath his arm. As much as I did not like to admit it, he really was quite handsome.

"Well, hello there," he said as we approached, a smile growing on his face as his eyes fell on William. "And there he is. My word, it is a relief to see him here, happy and healthy."

Felix and I stopped beside Eugene as William continued down the wide steps to the garden to chase after a pair of ducks making their way toward the lake. "I take it you just heard the news?" Felix asked.

"Yes," Eugene said. "Only just. In fact, I was about to rush over here to the estate to inform you of a rumor I'd heard, thinking it to be just what you would need to find the lad."

"Oh?" I asked. "You heard who took him?"

Eugene nodded. "Yes, talk finally made its way through to some of my connections, though the specific knowledge of William's kidnapping is still quite secret."

"And we would like to keep it that way," Richard said, coming over to stand with us.

"Mr. Sansbury," Eugene said, holding his hand out. "It is very good to meet you properly, sir."

"Likewise," Richard said. "I have heard you in concert. Quite remarkable."

"You are too kind, sir," Eugene said.

"How is the new eyesight?" Richard asked. "Still working well since the surgery?"

"Indeed," he said. "I think my vision might even be better than it was when I was a boy."

The two men laughed together like they were old friends.

"I do apologize for interrupting your gathering," Eugene said. "But when I heard the rumors I did, I rushed over here as quickly as I could."

"Rumors?" Richard asked. "About William, I take it?"

"Yes," Eugene said. "I had caught wind of a rumor

about a particular person being seen with your son, but before I left my family's property this very morning, I learned that Lillian and Felix had already resolved the matter and that William was back safe and sound with you."

"Yes, and thank God he is," Richard said with a visible sigh of relief. "Where did you learn of this?"

"Well, I learned of their uncovering the truth about the death of one of your servants, which is all that the newspapers have been reporting it as," Eugene said. "I realize, as you said, that you wish to keep William's part in it unknown."

Richard nodded. "My son has been through enough. I do not need half of London to know he was kidnapped."

"That makes sense to me," Eugene said. "Well, I am glad that he has been found, and is home. How is he handling it all?"

"Well enough, I suppose," Richard said. "I've hardly been able to sleep since he's been back, checking on him constantly. I've actually had a servant stand guard at his door all night in case he needs something or wakes frightened." He shook his head. "I realize how ridiculous it sounds, but I worry that someone might crawl through the window in the dead of night, or that he will have a terrible nightmare and be inconsolable."

"You are a good father," Eugene said. "I'm sure one of the reasons why he seems so happy is that he knows he is safe here with you, and that you would do anything to protect him."

"Yes..." Richard said, his eyes finding the boy at once. "I hope he does."

"We also have not told him the extent of the danger," I

said to Eugene. "Yes, I fled with him, but I still do not think he realizes what, exactly, it was all about."

"I have yet to tell him of George's fate, either," Richard said. "The servant who was killed when William was taken. I...haven't had the heart."

My stomach dropped, and I looked at him in surprise. "He doesn't know?"

Richard shook his head. "Not yet."

"He hasn't asked?" Felix asked.

"I've been avoiding the answer," Richard said.

I shook my head.

"I know he suspects something, but I would rather him think I dismissed George or something more innocent than that he was murdered," Richard said, dropping his voice. "He does not need to know."

"If you want him to trust you, you must tell him the truth," Felix said.

I looked sidelong at him. Interesting that he would choose to talk of truth, given his lack of a desire to do so with me.

Richard sighed. "I will, just not right now," he said. "He's been home for three days. We are still trying to deal with the situation at large, with the police reports, the upcoming trial for the kidnapper...everything."

Yes, he had his hands full. "As he gets older, he will have questions about what happened to him and why," I said. "It's only natural."

"I know," Richard said, his tone displaying his thinning patience. "I know. For now, however, I am going to do what I can to help him adjust to being home. I know he has settled in again well enough, but I want to be sure he truly is all right."

"Of course," I said. "That certainly seems the wisest way to proceed."

Richard nodded, and looked over at Eugene again. "So am I to presume that you simply wished to come over and congratulate these two on a job well done?"

"Well, in a way, and also to introduce myself properly to you, sir," Eugene said. "I'd hoped I would have the chance to ask Felix and Lillian to come to my next concert in London in a few day's time. I am certain they could do with some downtime, as well, given their involvement in the matter."

Richard looked over at us. "Yes, I am certain they could. They have been holed up here since William's return, and I can't imagine they would miss a chance to hear you play. Am I right?" He looked at Felix and me.

"We would be happy to hear the famous Eugene Osbourn play at last," I said, smiling. "We have yet to have the chance, as your concert was canceled on the ship."

"Excellent. I have brought tickets for you," Eugene said, procuring them from his coat pockets, handing one to each of us. "Front and center, for my guests. There will be food and drink provided in a private lounge during the intermission, and of course, I'll be there to greet you when I am not up on the stage."

"That sounds lovely," I said. "It's been too long since we've had a chance to see a proper performance like this."

"Yes, thank you for inviting us," Felix said.

Eugene beamed. "Wonderful. And you, Mr. Sansbury, of course you and your family would all be invited as well –"

"No, no, that's quite all right," Richard said, holding his hands aloft, but he smiled. "I am grateful for the offer, of course, and perhaps soon we will take you up on it, but I think we have had far too much excitement for some time, and would like to enjoy the quiet life at home for awhile."

"Of course, I entirely understand," Eugene said. He grinned at Felix and I. "Shall I send a Rolls-Royce to pick you up?"

"No, that's – " Felix began.

"That's very kind of you to offer," I said, smiling. "We would *love* it."

I knew Richard would have let us take his own car and driver into town, but my cousin's taste in automobiles was decidedly unglamorous and, after all we had been through recently, I felt like being a little spoiled.

Yes, it would take some time to recover from our latest adventure, I told myself, glancing around at our cheerful surroundings, but we were already on our way. Before we knew it, all thoughts of death and danger would be far behind us.

I was certain of it.

2

———

"Your dress looks nice," Felix said. "I'm not sure if I told you or not."

"Thank you," I said, turning my eyes away from the window, and all the lights of London. "I'm surprised you noticed."

It was nearly six o'clock, and we were ten minutes or so from the theater in the heart of London where we were going to see Eugene Osbourn perform. He'd sent a car for us, just as he said he would.

I could not remember the last time I'd been so excited for an event. Back in New York we had been accustomed to rubbing elbows with the elite of society. Our father's position with his company had ensured we were often surrounded by some of the most prestigious people in town.

But since coming to London, where I had been promised these sorts of events, we had not been to one. Dinners, yes, but nothing like a night on the town. Not like the night that Felix and I were about to finally enjoy.

"Well, I noticed you were gone earlier," he said. "I assumed you went into town to meet that dress designer?"

My face colored. "No, Felix. I procured this dress from the back of my magic wardrobe," I said, glaring at him. "Yes, I went to meet the dress designer."

Felix looked out the window, entirely unaffected by my sarcasm. "You must have used a great deal of your allowance to purchase it, as fine as it is."

The color in my face darkened. What did he know? "How could it possibly matter to you how I spend my own money?" I asked. "I didn't ask you what your new dinner jacket cost."

He shrugged. "It's unusual for you not to discuss it with me, that's all."

I looked away, my jaw working. He might have been right about that, but I would not admit it, not even to myself.

It had been almost a week since that day Mr. Osbourn had visited during Richard's luncheon. Shortly after he had left, I'd gone into town to meet with a designer that Gloria and Marie, William's older sisters, often visited for special occasions.

I looked down at the burgundy evening gown, which was embellished with dark beads in a swirling design across the front. It had a scooped neck in front and back and its fitted design flared into a fishtail hem around my ankles. Paired with a strand of matching beads woven through my short, bobbed hair and draped across my forehead, I knew it looked both modern and elegant. I had loved it the moment the designer had shown me its twin in green, and had asked how soon it could be made in burgundy. As it turned out, it was ready by this morning.

"It looks nice with your dark hair," Felix said, with about as much feeling as a chair could muster.

I reached up and touched my hair, glowering at him. *That's what the designer said, too...*

Felix looked over at me again. "Did you want to impress Eugene?"

I narrowed my eyes at him. "I bought this for myself," I said. "It's been a long time since I've had a new dress."

Felix made a noise of agreement, and it irritated me all the more.

The distance that had formed between us seemed to be growing wider with each passing day. Neither of us wished to address it, though I knew full well that he was aware of the gap, too. Was it pride? Was it shame?

The Rolls-Royce slowed to a stop a few moments later, and the door opened soon after.

The theater, which stood in the center of a long street lined with trees, glowed brilliantly against the darkening sky. The heat of the summer had faded with the sun, and the cool evening breeze rustled the ends of my hair. I was grateful that I'd brought a black fur stole with me.

People clustered near the ticket window, and Eugene Osbourn's name was surrounded in lights.

The excitement buzzed in the air, and it sent shivers down my spine.

These were the sorts of occasions that I *lived* for, attending luxurious, exclusive events, in elegant surroundings.

Felix held his arm out to me, and gave me a small smile...which set me a bit more at ease.

"Let's enjoy ourselves tonight, shall we?" he asked. "After everything...I think we have earned a break."

I grinned. "We certainly have."

We strolled into the theater, aware of the many sets of eyes drawn from us to the expensive car behind us. My heart quickened with excitement as the gazes of some of the women, and even the men, drifted toward my dress. It stood out from the others, who looked as if they had all copied one another.

I smirked.

If this doesn't catch Eugene's eye, then –

I stopped myself. What was I thinking? Why did I care what he thought of what I was wearing?

As we entered the building, I looked around the large foyer, with its emerald green carpet and matching wallpaper, mahogany staircases, and golden statue of a long-dead composer in the center of a marble dais.

"It's charming," I said, looking at those who had chosen to purchase tickets to the concert. "But I would have thought that as prestigious as Eugene is, he would have been asked to perform at a larger venue."

"My word, you have a supreme talent for appearing to compliment while striking with the back of your hand," Felix said in a low voice.

I glared at him out of the corner of my eye. "If you *listened,* you would have understood that I meant Mr. Osbourn could do better. He deserves a larger audience."

Felix shrugged as we headed toward the ticket collector.

I looked around as we came to the end of the line, waiting to be let into the theater proper. "This place seems ancient," I said. "I wonder how long it's been here."

"It looks recently renovated to me," Felix said, looking up at the same pillars and paintings I was examining.

"That's not what I mean," I said, my annoyance returning. "We have been to some of the newest theaters in New York. This one looks as if it has been here for a long, long time."

"Then maybe it is an honor for Eugene to be asked to play here," Felix said. "Some of these older places have a reputation for only asking particular types to play or perform. As contemporary as Eugene is, this will likely prove to be a great boon to him."

"Right," I said, somewhat reluctantly, annoyed that he was trying to outdo me with the positivity. "It's a great honor for him, I'm sure."

We reached the ticket keeper, who looked our tickets over, and smiled at us. "Ah, yes, Mr. Osbourn informed me that you would be coming. Allow me to fetch one of my colleagues who will take you to your seats."

I smiled at him as his words drew looks from anyone nearby. "Thank you very much," I said.

The usher reappeared with another, who gestured up the green carpet to the doors. "Right this way, please," he said with a warm smile.

The seats that Eugene had selected for us were front and center, in the most ideal part of the theater, right beside the piano. As we settled into our seats, I could feel the eyes on the back of my head, wondering who in the world we were, this pair who knew Mr. Osbourn, who had been personally invited by him.

Ah, what wonderful fate led to our meeting on that ship. If only our parents knew that they were not sending us away to punish us, but to a newfound success, they might have kept us right where we were.

An uncomfortable thought rose in the back of my mind, though. *If we had remained at home, then we likely never would have had to endure the dangers we have been caught up in lately...*

That might have been true, but hadn't I learned so much? And not only that, but managed to build a reputation for myself? Was that not more profitable for me?

Yes. Yes it was.

"Good evening, you two."

I turned to see one of Cousin Richard's friends and his wife coming around the front of the seats toward us.

"Oh, good evening, Mr. Tesley," I said, smiling. "And Mrs. Tesley, of course."

The woman, rosy-cheeked and round of face, smiled genteelly, though her eyes flashed. "How interesting to find you both up here, at the front," she said. "Why, one might think that you are acquainted with Mr. Osbourn."

"We most certainly are," I said, beaming at her, relishing the recognition. "He invited us personally, came to see us at our cousin's estate."

Mrs. Tesley's eyes narrowed, and she looked up at her husband.

"Well, isn't that interesting?" Mr. Tesley said. "I've met the man once myself. An agreeable chap, I'd say."

"Indeed he is," I said.

"Yes, my sister and he are quite the item," Felix said, flipping open the program the usher had given us.

My heart jumped as I shot him a look, daring him to say more. He didn't even look up at me.

"Really?" Mr. Tesley asked. "That is intriguing. When did this begin?"

"Oh, my brother jests," I said, shaking my head.

"So you are not seeing him?" Mrs. Tesley asked.

"I – no, I wouldn't say *that*," I said, my cheeks flushing. "We have been out together a time or two. Dinner, and the like."

Mr. Tesley nodded, but his wife's brows rose as she looked away.

It frustrated me to no end that I did not know which option would be the better choice for me. Should I tell people that we were together? Or should I deny it?

What would Eugene want or say?

"It's still very new, we have only met recently," I added. I shrugged, but allowed a playful smile to appear on my face. "I suppose we will see what comes of it."

"Well, we wish you the best," Mrs. Tesley said.

The lights on the stage slowly flickered on, and Mr. Tesley glanced up at it.

"We won't keep you," he said with a tight smile. "We just stopped over to say hello."

And to make sure that you were seen with those of us sitting in the front. I'm on to you, Mr. Tesley.

"Of course," Felix said, holding his hand out. "It was a pleasure seeing you, sir. We will be certain to let our cousin know that you stopped to see us."

"Yes, please do," he said. "Good evening."

"Yes, good evening," his wife added.

They turned and made their way back toward their seats.

"Five minutes until the concert," Felix said, still browsing the program.

I snatched it out of his hand.

He looked placidly over at me, blinking. "May I have that back, please?"

"No," I said, glaring at him. "Not until you explain to me why you thought it was all right to throw me out to sea as you just did."

My brother looked at me, unconcerned. "I said nothing that wasn't true," he said.

I rolled my eyes. "Felix, you know *very well* that there is nothing happening between Eugene and me."

Felix chuckled. "All right, dear sister. If you say so."

My cheeks burned all the more. "This is ridiculous," I said under my breath. I tossed the program back into his lap. "Why must you insist on humiliating me?"

"I cannot for the life of me understand why you think that being paired with Osbourn would be so bad. If anything, I would have thought you would lean into the idea, even just to increase your reputation. I mean... otherwise, why would you have decided to wear the gown you are?"

I looked away, doing my best to hold my tongue. If people were still looking at me, then I didn't want them to see me angry.

I tried to smooth my expression, and instead looked up at the stage, expectant.

"I've already told you, I think he could be a good match for you," Felix said, folding his hands in his lap. "You are happy when you're with him, and whether or not you want to admit it, I think you are intrigued by him."

"I – " I said.

"You just don't want to admit it to yourself," Felix said.

"Don't want to admit it to myself..." I murmured, my nose wrinkling. "Talking to me as if I am a child."

"Not at all," Felix said, still as cool as a spring pond. "You're only afraid of getting hurt again."

The lights on the stage flickered again, and soon, the rest of the sconces around the theater, up and down the walls, all began to dim. With a swish, the velvet curtains drew back across the stage, revealing a beautiful, ebony grand piano.

I didn't have a chance to retort, as Eugene strode out onto the stage to the sound of hundreds of people applauding his appearance.

He wore a black tailcoat with a white waistcoat and bow tie. He waved to the audience, beaming as he stopped beside the piano.

The applause continued, and he mouthed the words, "Thank you, thank you," as he smiled, allowing everyone the chance to greet him.

His eyes turned down toward where Felix and I sat, and his grin widened further as he spotted us. He gave us a wave, which Felix quickly returned.

I did, as well, almost startled that he had noticed us despite knowing full well that he had been the one to give us the tickets. Something was different. Seeing him drenched in the lights of the stage, welcoming the applause from the audience, made him seem so different than the man I'd met on the ship, who I'd dined with, who came around to Richard's estate.

He took a seat at the piano bench, flipping the tail of his coat over the edge, settling in. He turned around to acknowledge the audience once more, leaning toward the golden microphone beside the piano.

"Good evening, ladies and gentlemen," he said. "Thank you all so much for coming tonight. This is my first performance since arriving in London, and it is my great delight to be able to play for you this evening."

The applause exploded around us again, along with a shrill whistle from someone near the back. Laughter followed.

"Thank you, thank you," Eugene said. "And, as you all can see, this is also my first performance since my eye correction surgery, which was successful."

Louder cheers, and Felix and I clapped along with them enthusiastically. That was truly good news, and it seemed that the response from the rest of the audience proved his prior fears wrong.

"I am appreciative of all your encouragement. As you can imagine, I worried how the news would be received. If you would like to hear a bit of a secret, playing has been more difficult now that I can see properly, as I am not used to watching the way my hands move. I've had to reteach myself *not* to look as I play."

Laughter came on cue. I found his comment interesting, as it was something I had not considered. More than that, though, I could see the tension in his shoulders, and the way his eyes darted all around the theater, as if not quite sure what to focus on.

Almost as if he had heard my thoughts, he turned to look down at me where I sat.

"I might not have had the courage to tell everyone about the surgery, if it were not for the encouragement of a new friend of mine. She helped to remind me that people are often very understanding, and might even be happy for me."

He shifted in his seat, but I was glad that his eyes were still fixed upon me. For a moment, it was as if he was speaking to me, and only to me.

"Thank you, Lillian, for helping me put my fears aside. I might have lived forever in that darkness, and who knows? Maybe I would have given up music entirely."

My face flushed, but I smiled up at him in return as applause then filled the theater...for me.

"Now...I have talked for too long," Eugene said. "All I ask is that you sit back, relax, and enjoy the music."

I had heard pianists play live before, and had been told that Eugene had talent, but to hear him play for the first time was nothing short of remarkable. For the first hour, I sat back in awe and simply listened, allowing the emotion and flow of the music to wash over me. He perfectly captured the feel of the pieces he had named and written himself, from *Serenity* to *Majesty*. Simple, but lovely. The frustration I'd felt, the annoyance I'd been carrying, and the worries and cares from the past few weeks washed away as I listened. By the time he stepped off the stage and the curtains closed once again for the intermission, I felt peace and serene calm unlike I'd felt in a very long time.

Felix questioned an usher about the lounge that Eugene had promised us, which the usher was all too eager to show us. It was a room made of windows, with views down into the foyer, and with plush furniture, sparkling, golden plates and crystal glasses. Everywhere, there were servers dressed in crisp shirts and the scent of dark chocolate and cinnamon permeated the air.

We found our way to an empty table near the

windows looking into the foyer. "Look at all the other guests down there," I said with a smirk. "All on top of one another like that, and here we are in this luxurious space with amazing food and drinks and people…"

Felix grinned. "Wouldn't Father be surprised to see this?"

"Mother would be furious," I said over the top of my crystal flute. "I cannot wait to write and tell her about it."

Felix smirked, popping a pitted cherry into his mouth.

I turned to see Eugene enter the room, and those that noticed him broke into applause. The couple closest to him approached, and he shook their hands enthusiastically.

"Hmm," I said. "Do you suspect that he invited all of us? Gave us all tickets?"

"Perhaps," Felix said. "But I think it is more likely that most of these people paid for this experience. These ticket levels are a great deal more expensive, and in limited quantity."

I continued to sip my drink as Eugene made his way around the room, until he came over to our table.

"The man of the hour," I said.

He grinned. "It is good to see you both. Thank you for coming."

"We are happy to be here," Felix said. "You are a fine pianist, Eugene. It has been a pleasure to watch you play."

"Yes, it certainly has," I said. "It has been wonderful."

His smile warmed. "Well, thank you both very much," he said. "It is always my supreme joy to hear that my audience enjoys my playing."

"And you have written all of those pieces yourself?" I asked.

He nodded. "I did. But I feel as if I have a different relationship with them now that I can see. They were all written by simply hearing the notes. Now...my mind tends to imagine new things as opposed to what it used to."

"Oh?" I asked. "Such as?"

"Well..." he said, and his smile became sheepish.

"It's you," Felix said, matter of fact. "He thinks of you now, I'll bet."

My cheeks burned, and I resisted the urge to toss the rest of my drink in my brother's face. I laughed, shooting him a look as I did. "Oh, Felix. You're *so funny.*"

Eugene laughed as well. "I really came over to let you both know of the party taking place after the concert this evening," he said. "I do not know if either of you are acquainted with Mr. Tesley, but he has offered his home just a few blocks away from here."

"Oh, Mr. Tesley," I said. "Yes, we know him. He is friends with Richard."

Eugene smiled. "I might have guessed. Well, I wanted to pass along the invitation to you both. You would be more than welcome."

"Thank you very much," I said, and glanced over at Felix. "What do you think?"

Felix shrugged, looking at Eugene. "Will there be cards?"

"This is London, isn't it?" Eugene asked. "Of course."

"Then count me in," Felix said with a grin.

"Excellent," Eugene said. "Now, if you'll excuse me, I

need to get backstage again. My producer will be furious if I'm late for curtain call."

I lifted a brow. "I'm surprised you let anyone push you around, Eugene."

"If he didn't, then I would be like an aimless duck, I'm afraid," he said. "I'll see you two later."

I watched him leave, feeling a bizarre desire to go after him.

I had loved my former fiancé, Thomas Williams. I had agreed to marry him at one point, hadn't I? I thought he was good looking, and charming, and I enjoyed his company.

Then why was it that something felt so vastly different when I was around Eugene? How could it be different? I had already known what love was like.

The warmth in my chest continued to spread pleasantly as I saw him disappear around the corner. It had to be his fame, and the thrill of being associated with him. Surely that was all it was.

"I don't know why you keep lying to yourself," Felix said, as if reading my mind.

My head snapped toward him, and I glared. "Not a word out of you," I said.

A bell toned from somewhere down in the foyer, and Felix got to his feet. "All right, come on. Let's not miss the curtain."

I followed after my twin, keeping a careful eye on him as we went.

I wondered when the dam would break, so to speak, and we would have to confront this growing tension between us. If it carried on for much longer, I was certain we would end up alienating ourselves from one another, simply because it was easier to leave things as they were. I did not care much for the idea, but if he continued to treat me as he was, or if I continued to ignore the festering wound that had been our prior conversation, then there would be little I could do. Little either of us could do.

I never would have imagined a time in my life that Felix and I would have been standing on opposing sides. I had never once had to question his support, even at times when I was heading toward foolishness. I never abandoned him, either.

There are lines, though. Boundaries must be maintained. Am I supposed to follow him if he chooses to gamble with his life?

No, of course I wasn't. If he was ever going to do something stupid, then it was my place to try and stop him, to bring him to his senses. Who else would he listen to?

Then where were you the night Danny died?

The question I kept returning to, the same blame that Felix must have been wrestling with, took hold of my heart and squeezed so tight it made my head swim. I kept thinking that if I had been there, I could have prevented... whatever it was that happened. Felix would have had help, Daniel would have had more eyes to watch him.

As we reclaimed our seats, I tried to put on an indifferent face. These questions and reflections meant nothing, in the end. It wasn't as if they would bring Daniel back from the grave. He'd been dead for so many years now.

Was it truly possible that Felix was personally responsible? That he had somehow played a deliberate part in our brother's death?

The lights dimmed around us, bathing us in cool shadows, dampening the conversation to a quiet murmur before the last of the voices faded away entirely.

Eugene reappeared on the stage, and his quick glance so pointedly in my direction made me reconsider Felix's words I had so quickly brushed aside. Was he right, when he said that Eugene thought of me, as he played? That seemed...

I couldn't quite make up my mind how it made me feel, as the music began. Flattered, certainly.

Just as Eugene had begun the second song of his set, a disturbance behind us caused me to turn and look over my shoulder.

A man shimmied along his row, passing by other guests as quickly as he could in order to reach the aisle. He nearly stumbled over the arm of the last seat before racing up the carpeted aisle, apologizing to guests as he made his way along.

I rolled my eyes, turning back to the stage.

"Drunk?" Felix leaned over to ask me.

"Likely," I answered. "Heading to the washroom, I'm sure."

He nodded and returned his attention to the music.

Another song passed, and a commotion seemed to be forming at the back of the room. Whispers had started to grow, with tones of question. I turned around once more, ready to scold them all for ruining the peace and quiet of the theater, when I looked in time to see some of the attendants at the back hurrying out to the foyer.

The murmur of the crowd grew as people turned entirely around in the chairs, some even getting to their feet. A group of men strode back into the theater, and soon after, chirps of voices cascaded down to the front row like the tide washing in.

The same questions were being asked, sending a chill down my spine.

"Dead?"

"What do they mean?"

"Someone is actually dead? But how?"

3

"Edmund Culpepper," I read, taking lazy, slow steps before the fireplace, reading the article prominently printed on the front page of the morning newspaper. "It seems that couple we heard speculating before we left the theatre were right."

It was late morning the following day. Felix sat in the chair near the window, his gaze sweeping the lake outside as a flock of geese landed gracefully on the glassy surface. Richard sat at his desk, a stack of business papers or some such piled on one side of the polished surface. He'd been putting it off for almost a week, celebrating William's return. Unfortunately, it now begged his return to his duties.

He looked up, his pen poised over a signature line. "Culpepper, you say?" he asked.

"Why am I not at all surprised that you know him?" I asked, looking up over the top of the paper at him.

Richard smiled slightly. It seemed his sense of humor

was slowly returning. "I have many connections in my line of work."

"What does the rest of the article say?" Felix asked from his place at the window.

I looked down once again at the paper. "Well...it gives the man's biography and history, for starters," I said. "Says here he was the youngest son of a Sir William Culpepper, a prominent land owner to the north of London."

"That's true," Richard said. "His father is a wealthy and powerful man."

"Then much of his family's wealth is inherited?" I asked.

"Indeed," Richard said. "Though our deceased Mr. Culpepper would hardly have seen any of it. Most would probably be going to his eldest brother when their father passes, and likely some to his sisters for their marriages."

"That explains why the article goes on to say he was a barrister?" I asked. "But a rather influential one, by the sound of it, one of the wealthiest, given the cases he chose to take."

Richard nodded. "You might think it a surprise that I knew him, but he was well-known by many in the city. He made a name for himself in a rather...unconventional manner."

"...*He had a tendency to take on extraordinary cases,*" I read, pausing in front of the crackling fire. "*Even those that seemed entirely outlandish, with great success.*"

"Precisely," Richard said, looking back down at his papers, signing his name upon them.

"Does the article describe what happened last night?" Felix asked.

I quickly scanned the piece. "Hardly," I said. "Apart

from mentioning that he was found dead in the foyer in the middle of a concert, and that it is believed he died from some sort of heart condition, there is nothing."

Felix folded his hands in his lap, twirling his thumbs around one another in an infinite chase. "I cannot say I am surprised," he said. "I heard more than one person last night say the same, that he must have had a health condition. It was even speculated that he had driven himself to poor health, taking on such difficult work."

"What happened last night?" Richard asked. "He was simply found on the floor, out in the foyer?"

"Yes, that is essentially the whole of it," I said with a shrug. "We came out to see what all the excitement was about, as did many others, and people had crowded around him. He had no visible injuries. It looked like he had just...collapsed."

"See? Likely health troubles," Felix said.

"Although..." I said.

"No," Felix said, turning around to look at me, shaking his head. "No, Lillian, do not try to make more of this than what it is."

"I am not making more of anything," I said, glaring at him. "All I was going to say is that while we were watching the concert, before he died, I saw a man scurry out of the theater as quickly as he could, as if he thought he might be sick."

Felix narrowed his eyes. "Do you think it was Mr. Culpepper?"

"It was dark in the theater, so I cannot say," I said. "I thought he looked familiar, but I cannot be sure. Besides, it isn't as if it matters if I saw him alive so soon before he died. His family or friends that were there with him could attest to the same thing, I'm sure. It isn't as if it would give any further clue as to how he died, simply narrowing down the time that he likely perished."

Felix sighed, his expression hardening. "You are starting to see suspicious deaths around every corner," he said. "That is not normal, and you know it."

I glared at him. "Let me think...well, aboard the ship, we witnessed a murder. Then, one of our cousin's servants was *also* murdered. Then a man randomly drops dead at a concert, a young man, mind you? Forgive me, Felix, for thinking that it might be following along the same pattern of our lives as of late."

"It's nothing more than coincidence..." Felix said with a dismissive wave of his hand, turning to look back out the window.

"Coincidence. Really?" I asked, planting my hands on my hips. "I will have you know that I – "

The door to the study opened, and William and his two older sisters came in.

"Father, what are they talking about?" William asked, striding right over to his father's desk.

Richard's eyes widened slightly, and he quickly tried to settle his face into a smile. "It's nothing to be concerned about, son," he said. "It is of no trouble to us."

William turned his blue eyes to Felix. "Did something happen at the concert last night?"

Felix looked at me, and I shrugged, rolling my eyes as I turned away.

"It's...complicated, Will," Felix said. "What matters is that everything is fine."

"Is it fine for the family of the man who died?"

Gloria leaned against the door, her arms crossed, eyes narrow slits.

The eldest of Richard's children, Gloria was near my age, but often behaved far younger, with a liking for theatrics and a tendency to quarrel with her slightly younger sister Marie.

I wanted to tell Gloria now that she shouldn't keep such a pretty face in such a nasty expression, but refrained.

William's face crumpled, and he took a step closer to his father.

"Gloria, now is not the time," her father said in a low, warning tone.

Gloria rolled her eyes. "How long are you going to shield him, Father? You haven't even told him the full truth about what happened when he was kidnapped."

My heart beat more quickly as I looked at her. "What's with the bone picking?" I asked.

Gloria's head shot toward me, but she didn't retaliate. Instead, she nodded at the paper in my hand. "Did I hear you say the name of the man was Mr. Culpepper?"

"Were you standing outside the door, listening?" Richard asked.

"We didn't know that you didn't want us to hear..." William said in a nervous voice.

Richard sighed. "It isn't...never mind. Yes, Gloria. It was Mr. Culpepper."

Gloria's eyes flashed. "What happened to him?"

My own expression hardened. "From the look on your face, I might have to assume that you knew him?"

Marie gave her older sister an anxious look. It seemed I was correct.

"Not me, personally..." Gloria said with a nonchalant shrug that seemed entirely contrary to her sharp stare. "A friend of mine was courted by him at one point in time, though."

My brows rose. "A former relationship?" I asked. "I take it that things did not go so well?"

"No, because from what I've heard, he was an utter idiot," Gloria snapped. "Nothing more than a handsome face."

"What happened?" I asked.

"All she told me was that he was a heartless fiend," she said with a shrug. "She despises the mention of his name. Whatever it was that he said, or did, it was unforgivable in her eyes."

"I know from experience that he was a rather disagreeable fellow, yes," Richard said. "Remember that he took on only the most extreme cases as a barrister."

"That should tell you all you need to know about him," Gloria said. "I only ever met him once, at a ball with the same friend I mentioned. He was not very attentive to my friend. His eyes followed all the attractive women in the room, and he would wander away on a whim whenever the fancy struck him."

"Sounds like the sort who lived high and happily in his circles," Felix said. "I know the type."

I said, "Which leads me to believe, even more so, that it might have been – "

"Whatever he was like, it doesn't mean someone killed him," Felix said, cutting me off. "Besides...even if something about the whole business was askew, what would it matter to you? You don't need to worry about it. It doesn't concern us. Right?"

My eyes narrowed, and I pursed my lips. "My, how nice of you to join us, *Father*."

Felix's face darkened in response, and he turned away.

The sickly sweetness of successfully putting him in his place gave me the fuel to round on Gloria again. "Are you trying to tell me that you think someone might have done something to him?"

"I don't know," Gloria said. "But Felix is right. Why does it matter if they did? Do you plan to go out there and try to get to the bottom of it again?"

I bristled. "In case you've forgotten, it was because of my efforts that we were able to figure out who took your brother – "

"Your efforts *and* mine," Felix corrected.

"Yes, but am I not the one who went and got him out of the building? I do have the injury to prove it," I said, holding my wrist aloft, before remembering it had healed enough that it was no longer wrapped.

Richard set his pen down, and rose from his seat again. "Come along, William. It's time for your archery lessons."

"Right now?" William asked. "But I want to – "

"I'm sorry, William, We need to go," Richard said.

I might have missed the warning glance that Richard shot me as he and William left the room if another figure had not stepped into the doorway.

It was Hughes, and the butler's eyes fell upon me at once.

"Miss Crawford, Mr. Crawford, Mr. Osbourn is here to see you both," he said.

Felix looked over at me, rising from his seat. "I hope everything is all right," he said in a low voice.

We said nothing to one another as we made our way toward the foyer. My heart drummed in my chest as I wondered what in the world could possibly have gone wrong now to bring this particular visitor to us so unexpectedly. Despite my interest mere moments ago, I suddenly found myself hoping that I was wrong about Mr. Culpepper's death plunging us into the midst of some new trouble.

We found Eugene Osbourn just inside the door, his coat speckled with raindrops, his dark hair pushed to the side and clinging to his forehead from what must have been a sweep of his hand.

"Oh, good," he said, upon seeing us, his face relaxing. "I am sorry for coming on such short notice. After everything that happened last night, I felt just terrible and knew that I must come and apologize to you."

"Eugene, you did not need to come all the way out here to see us," I said. "It isn't your fault that something happened."

"No, but I feel terrible that it happened during my performance," he said.

"If he had not been at the concert hall, he likely would still have died anywhere else he might have been," Felix said. "No one blames you."

Eugene's face fell, and he swept some more of his wet hair from near his brow. "My debut in London...and someone had to get hurt."

"From what the papers said, he suffered from a heart condition," Felix said. "Which I also heard from some of the other guests there last night."

The muscles in Eugene's jaw tightened, and he looked down. "Even so, I imagine there will be many people who will always think of the death that happened at my show. If the attendance at my performances does not suffer, I will be greatly surprised."

"It seems out of character for you to worry about ticket sales," I said.

Eugene looked at me in question. "That is not at all what I am concerned about. I am worried for my audience, that it might taint their experience of music or concerts in general. I don't want anyone to hear a piano now and think of someone falling dead in the foyer. It happened at my concert. It is, in a way, my responsibility."

Felix shook his head. "Nonsense," he said. "You are needlessly punishing yourself for something that was out of your control. How could you have known anything like that was going to happen?"

"I have wondered if I should make a public statement, giving my condolences to the family of the deceased," Eugene said. "I am a public figure, and there might be expectations for me to do something of the sort."

"I think you might be thinking about all this too much," I said. "I cannot imagine the family is sitting about, worrying because you haven't said anything to them yet."

"You're right," he said, though he did not seem at all relaxed about it. "More than anything, I can understand the depth of their grief right now. To have received such news so suddenly – "

The crunch of gravel in the drive drew my attention, and I looked out the open door to see a handsome car pulling up to the manor. Unfamiliar as it was, the gleam of the dark paint and the shine of the metallic accents told me that it could not have been more than a few weeks old at best, and likely cost a fortune.

"Who might this be?" I asked in a murmur.

After coming to a stop, the chauffeur hopped out of the front and hurried around to the back to open the door for his passenger.

A tall woman stepped out, her reddish blonde hair swirled up into an elegant coil on the top of her head, adorned with a trio of emerald pins that matched the deep green of her elaborate dress. A dark veil covered her face, and her expression appeared like stone as she marched up the steps toward the open front door.

"My word..." she said, her nose wrinkling behind her lacey veil. "Why do people in the country insist upon leaving their doors and windows open? Do they not realize how filthy it is?"

I folded my arms as she stepped through the door, uninvited, and opened my mouth to speak when Hughes appeared and bowed to her. "Good morning, madam – "

"Mrs. Burke, thank you," the woman said shortly. "I am looking for a Lillian Crawford. Is she here?"

"I am," I said, stepping around the butler, my eyes narrowing. "To what do I owe the pleasure?"

Her green eyes flashed like the emeralds in her hair as she lowered her chin. "I hear that you solve crimes, and I am in need of your services."

4

I blinked at her, startled for a moment, but then realized I shouldn't be surprised. Newspaper articles about the death aboard ship, and the more recent murder of Richard's servant, had named me as the one to discover the perpetrators of both crimes. Small wonder if strangers now felt they could approach me about their own troubles, in search of solutions.

Of course, the reasonable thing would be to explain to this woman that I was no professional investigator and send her away. But curiosity got the better of me, and I made a snap decision to hear her out.

"Perhaps something can be arranged," I said vaguely. "Why don't you come with me? We can have a chat, discuss the – "

"My brother was murdered," she snapped, fixing a cool gaze on me, utterly ignoring the men around us. "And I demand to know who did it."

My brows rose, and I stared at her. "Well, I might be

good at what I do, but I cannot procure the answer out of thin air as you *demand*."

"Do not trifle with me," she said.

"Who is trifling with whom?" I asked. "You came to see *me,* did you not? Yet you come in here and act as though you are somehow the one in charge – "

"I am the one in charge," she said plainly, without an ounce of courtesy.

My mouth hung open for a minute before Felix stepped up beside me.

"Good morning, ma'am," he said. "My name is Felix Crawford. I have assisted my sister in her...um, investigations."

Mrs. Burke appeared unimpressed. "This is a ridiculous waste of time," she said. "I should have known better than to – Mr. Eugene Osbourn?"

Eugene looked side to side, seeming surprised to find himself noticed. "Yes?" he asked.

She stopped, staring around at all three of us, her demeanor like that of a ruffled bird. She glared at me pointedly, before speaking again. "It is quite strange that you are here, Mr. Osbourn, given my very reason for coming. I have no choice but to admit that this must be fate."

My heart churned in my chest. "You are here about Mr. Culpepper."

Felix and Eugene turned to look at me just as Mrs. Burke did as well.

"Yes, I am," she said. "He is...*was* my brother."

"I see," I said. "And you suspect that he was murdered?"

"I have no other reason for being here, do I?" she demanded.

"Why don't you come in and have a seat?" Felix asked. "Hughes, would you be so kind as to fetch us tea?"

"Certainly," Hughes said, and started toward the kitchen.

Our guest followed the rest of us to the drawing room at the end of the hall. Felix ducked away for a moment to inform Richard that we had a visitor, and Eugene stayed with me.

Mrs. Burke found the best chair in the room at once, with a view out over the lake, and sat down in it. I assumed the chair across from her, giving her a cool look as I did.

"Why are you here, Mr. Osbourn?" she asked, turning her face up to him. This close, I could see she was likely in her late forties, perhaps a bit older. She must have been stunning in her youth, with those brilliant green eyes and that tall frame. Her attitude, however, certainly left a great deal to be desired.

"I was simply paying my friends a visit," Eugene answered with a tight smile. "Though I am beginning to wonder, as well, if I was destined to be here for a greater reason this morning. Mrs. Burke, might I begin by saying how terribly sorry I am for your loss?"

She looked at him, her face as blank and cold as steel. "I have no need for your condolences," she said. "They are as useful to me as stones."

He seemed taken aback. "I only mean to say that – "

"You feel guilty that it occurred at your performance last night," she said without looking up at him again.

"You feel as if the timing makes what happened your fault."

Felix reentered the room, and his eyes narrowed as soon as he heard her words. He looked over at me, and I could almost hear his thoughts.

Who does this woman think she is?

"That is rather self-centered of you," she went on. "To think of the death of my brother as if it were all about you."

Eugene's brow furrowed, and he looked confused. "Mrs. Burke, I can assure you that I only – "

"I do not care what or who you are," she said, quite simply. "Unless you are the one who murdered him, then I have no need for you. Yes, your concert happened to be the vehicle that was used to kill him, but it might have been anywhere else. You are not responsible, so do not try and garner any pity from me."

I blinked at her, nearly as stunned as Eugene must have felt.

She turned her attention back to me. "To be perfectly frank, I am only coming to you because I read in the papers how you managed to solve that elaborate murder on the ocean liner recently, and because the police refuse to get involved in this. They say there is simply no evidence of my brother's death being suspicious, telling me that I am mistaken for thinking it anything more than a natural death." She shook her head. "Well, I knew my brother and his reputation, and as such, I know full well that I am *not* mad for assuming otherwise."

I looked over at Felix, who had pulled a deck of cards from his pocket, and sitting at a nearby table, had begun to shuffle them. Eugene seemed uncertain whether to join him or stay near me.

"I realize I may have chosen the wrong investigator, given there are so many in London," she went on. "But you seem to come to solutions quickly, and from what I read, the case on that ship was bizarre and rather ridiculous."

"That it was," I said. "I have resolved another, similar matter since then, you might be interested to hear – "

" – And my brother dealt with the bizarre and ridiculous, so if for nothing more than to try and expedite the process, I thought it best to come to you first and see what you could offer me," she finished, apparently not hearing a word I'd said.

I blinked at her, annoyance bubbling just beneath the surface.

When I looked back at Felix, he seemed entirely disinterested, the way that he stacked and unstacked the cards in his hands. I knew better, however. He was most certainly listening.

Why do I care what he thinks? He has clearly proven that he does not want to listen to what I have to say. How can I trust him in these matters? How can I possibly rely on his opinion?

"I will pay you a fair rate," said Mrs. Burke. "And expect the whole affair to be resolved within the week. The funeral is in a few days, the preparations have already begun, and I do not want to dawdle at getting to the truth."

"Well, I would be happy to speak with you about all of these matters," I said, trying to maintain a calm tone. "Though I suppose the first place to start would be at the beginning, wouldn't it? Why do you believe it to have been a murder?"

She rolled her eyes. "I have already told you, the police gave me a great deal of grief about – "

"You have already told me that they chased you off, I know," I said. "I am not asking if you believe it was murder. I am asking *why* you think it was murder. What happened that makes you think so?"

"He was behaving...strangely," she said.

"Pardon me, ma'am, but there were many who were there at the concert last night who said that your brother suffered from an unfortunate malady," Eugene said, cautiously. "A heart condition, or some such."

"Indeed," Felix said. "Those issues often come with a sudden onset."

She shook her head. "No, he did not simply drop dead of some heart problem," she said, her tone seeming a bit unfeeling to be discussing her own brother. "It was something he drank, I am certain of it."

"Drank? Why drank specifically?" I asked.

"He was sent a drink from a 'Secret Admirer' last night. It would not be the first time, by any stretch of the imagination, so I hardly noticed. But it is the only thing I can think of that was different than usual."

"How often would you say he was sent these gifts out in public places?" I asked.

"Not always, of course," she said. "That was perhaps the third or fourth time I was present for it."

"I assume he claimed it happened more frequently?" I asked.

"He said it was nearly every time he dined out," she said. "But he was always prone to exaggerating..."

"What was it about last night that was different?" Eugene asked.

"I...don't know," she said. "He was especially boastful last night – again, not terribly shocking – but he was nearly insufferable, had been for some weeks. It seemed a case he had been working had gone extremely well, and he was highly pleased with himself over it."

She hesitated. "The drink came at such a strange moment," she continued. "Just before the bell sounded for us to return to the theater. Ordinarily, when admirers sent him drinks, the givers made themselves known. But last night, the giver remained anonymous."

"There could be many explanations for that," I said. "They could have stepped out of the room for a variety of obvious and understandable reasons."

"No," she said. "A rather large show was made of the whole thing, drawing annoyed stares from those closest to us. It...well, frankly, it unsettled me. Something about the whole delivery, the timing, the drink itself...it did not seem right. I told him my concerns, warned him not to drink it. He didn't seem to care. As flattered and full of himself as he was in the moment, he drank it happily."

"Did he show symptoms of being ill right then?" Eugene asked.

I shook my head for her. "I imagine not. It wasn't until after the show began again that he got up and fled the auditorium," I said.

Her eyes flashed. "You saw him leave? You were there?"

I gestured toward Felix. "We were sitting in the front as Mr. Osbourn's guests," I said. "I heard your brother get up, saw him rush out. I thought nothing of it at the time, but upon seeing who it was in the foyer... His photograph was in the paper this morning and I recognized him as the man from the theatre."

She scowled, shaking her head. "That drink is what killed him. I am convinced of it."

"The timing does seem suspicious," Felix said lazily from the table. "A poison could be slow-acting, and take some time to work. How long had it been since he finished the drink to when you sat down?"

"No more than ten minutes or so," Mrs. Burke said.

Felix nodded as he laid a card down, though he said no more.

"So all you have to go on so far is that you believe his drink was poisoned?" I asked. "And the person who sent it to him is the killer?"

"That's correct," she said. "Apart from that, I have little information."

I drew in a deep breath, and let it out in a huff. "Well, I will certainly do what I can."

"So, you'll take the job?" she asked.

I didn't need to think about it. Right from the beginning, this death had intrigued me.

"Yes," I said. "I'll take it."

"Good," Mrs. Burke said, getting to her feet at once. "Then I expect you to be at my family's estate tomorrow at noon, sharp. There you will have the chance to meet our family, and collect whatever information you need in order to begin your investigating."

"Very well," I said.

"I shall leave the address with the doorman on my way out," she said.

"That will be fine," I said. *Though I do not imagine Hughes will be too pleased to be called a doorman.*

She strolled out of the drawing room, and the *clack* of her heels against the floor faded as she disappeared down the hall.

"I think we should have discussed whether or not to get involved in this business before agreeing to it," Felix said, breaking the silence.

I turned to him. "Oh? And why is that?"

My twin gave me a hard look. "Do you really want to become entangled in yet another murder?" he asked.

"Yes. I thought that would be obvious by my agreeing to it," I said, planting my hands on my hips. "In case you haven't noticed, I am rather good at investigating. I seem to have discovered a skill I never knew I had."

Felix shook his head. "That's not the point. We should have discussed whether it is wise for you and I to – "

"What is there to talk about?" I asked, the annoyance growing within me.

"Well, it certainly is not as if we need the money," Felix said.

"I agree, we do not need the money," I said. "That isn't why I accepted. It is the fact that I *can* earn money in this way. The novelty of using my skills and intelligence to earn income is appealing, but I suppose you wouldn't understand that. Anyway, I am fascinated by it all, and rather enjoy the strategic solving of the crimes."

"I don't mean to intrude, but you do seem to have a knack for this sort of thing," Eugene said. "It's unlike anything I've ever witnessed. You must give her that, Felix."

Felix shot him a look, but said nothing.

"And if you could help this woman and her family, isn't that what is most important?" Eugene asked. "To get justice for everyone involved?"

"Yes, helping the victim's family, of course," I said, less enthusiastically. "That is naturally another reason why I accepted."

Eugene must have detected my lack of sincerity, for he looked over at me and seemed surprised for a moment. "I realize the reason you solved the case on the ship was because you were dragged in," he said. "And with your cousin's murdered servant, it was a personal family matter. But this time, you are entirely uninvolved, apart from the fact that you happened to be there when the death occurred, correct?"

"I would be interested in taking this sort of case even if I were entirely separated from it," I said.

"You might think the reason you want to do this is just to prove you can," Eugene said. "But I can see that you take pride in helping people. You have realized the good in doing what only you can do."

I looked up at him, studying him. "Mr. Osbourn, I do not know if you are an utter fool, or somehow keenly perceptive about a side of me that I do not know."

He grinned at me.

"Are you truly certain you want to dabble with all this muck and mire again?" Felix asked.

I could see the worry in his eyes, but for some reason, in that moment, it only increased the determination in my own.

"Yes. I do."

5

The Culpepper estate sat just outside the city of London, raised up on a nearby hill where part of the city's harbor remained in view.

"You know, it's amazing how small their property is," I said, looking around. "I can see every square inch of it. The house is impressive, yes, but look how close their neighbors are."

"Yes, it's unexpected, isn't it?" Felix said, gazing out the window of the car.

"Given the way Mrs. Burke was going on yesterday, I would have assumed their family's estate would have been more impressive."

"She certainly gave you a run for your money," Felix said.

I turned and glared at him. "What do you mean by that?"

He shrugged. "You and she are a great deal alike, all things considered."

"And how is that?" I asked.

"I don't know if I can explain it to you," he said. "You're very proud, and so is she. I might have thought the two of you would get along, but perhaps you are too much alike."

"That woman is bitter and rude," I said. "Are you implying I am the same?"

"Not all the time," Felix said.

I glared at him as the car pulled to a stop.

The home of the dead man's family was grand and ancient looking, made entirely of stone and lead-paned windows. Pillars held up the crescent terrace overhang above the front steps, where marble benches stood awaiting their next guests, and ivy snaked up the sides of the tower on the eastern end of the building.

We were greeted at the door by the family butler, who introduced himself as Mr. Fawkes. "Mrs. Burke is here, waiting," he said in a nasally voice. "She told me to expect you."

"Thank you," I said, strolling in.

The foyer was bright and open, with many windows that poured the summer light in. The place was handsomely furnished and decorated, though with more of a French country house feel, rather than English. I appreciated the yellow and blue color scheme, all the same.

"It would be lovely...if it weren't for the wailing," I said under my breath to Felix as the butler took us toward the back sunroom to meet with the family.

We soon found the source of the wretched sound, which happened to be coming from a woman who looked like a slightly older version of Mrs. Burke, seated in an elaborately upholstered chair surrounded by seven other people. She wore all black, dress, hat and veil. Her gloved hands nearly covered her face, and clutched the only bit of color to her face, a bright blue handkerchief that she blew her nose noisily into.

A plain looking man stood behind her, of average height and build, wearing a dark suit and an entirely unpleasant expression as the woman in the chair before him continued to sob hysterically into her hands.

"Miss Crawford," came the sharp tone of Mrs. Burke, who stood to her feet like a heron straightening its legs and feathers. "Mr. Crawford, too, I see."

She strode over to us where we stood at the door, her bright green eyes flashing as they fell upon us.

"Mrs. Burke," I said. "How do you do?"

"Lovely, thank you for asking," she answered in a dry tone. She turned and gestured around the room. "This is my family. To the left here is my eldest brother, Mr. Theodore Culpepper and his wife, Elizabeth. To his left is our sister, Miss Margaret. You see my father there, behind the chair, Sir Culpepper, and my mother, Lady Culpepper. Beside them is our other sister, now the youngest in our family, Mrs. Newman and her husband, Mr. Victor Newman. And then at the end is my husband, Mr. Henry Burke."

It did not seem that more than two or three had noticed their introductions being given.

"I informed them that you were coming," Mrs. Burke said, crossing her long, thin arms, eyeing the others in the sunroom. "Mother did not take it well."

The woman in the upholstered chair cried even louder, as if in protest.

"Poor woman," Felix said. "To lose her son…"

"It's – it's *terrible!*" the woman wailed. "How can I go *on*?"

"There, there, darling..." said Sir Culpepper, gently patting his wife's shoulder.

"My boy..." the woman cried into her handkerchief. "My *baby* boy!"

"She's been like this since I came home that night from the theatre," Mrs. Burke said. "She hasn't eaten, and only slept when she simply had no strength to go on – "

"Why, oh *why* did he ever go to that theatre?" Lady Culpepper cried. "How will I ever be happy again?"

This is beginning to feel more like a performance than real grief...

"Mr. and Miss Crawford," said Mr. Burke, getting up and coming to greet us. He was a tall man, with dark brown hair and a thick, bristly moustache. "Thank you for coming."

"We are happy to help," Felix said.

"Yes, indeed," I said, looking around. "Well, shall we begin? I do not wish to intrude on your...grief for too long."

Lady Culpepper continued to sob into her hands.

"My apologies, but what did you say?" asked Mr. Culpepper, Mrs. Burke's brother. "I do not wish to be rude." He got up as well, and started toward us.

"I said – " I began.

"Come along, darling," said Sir Culpepper, reaching down to hook his hand beneath his wife's arm.

She seemed to hardly notice as he pulled her from the chair, leading her from the room.

"This will trouble her too much," he said to Mr. Culpepper and Mrs. Burke as they passed by.

"Of course," Mr. Culpepper said, standing aside to let them go.

They headed back out into the hall, and Lady Culpepper's cries faded as they made their way down the corridor.

"She does not approve of me hiring you," Mrs. Burke said sharply, her eyes narrow slits as she stared out into the empty hall. "Tells me it is outrageous to assume anything so terrible happened to him."

"She is simply surprised that he died in the first place," said Mr. Culpepper. "As are we all, of course."

"Perfectly understandable," I said. "I can see how she would be so distraught. It was her son, after all."

"Parents should not have to bury their children," Felix said in a low voice.

"No," Mr. Culpepper agreed. "They most certainly should not."

"You said you had some questions for us," Mrs. Burke said, stepping in again. "Why don't you come and join us? It would be better for us all to sit. We have not had a great deal of rest with our mother the way she is."

Felix and I found seats amongst the family members. The visit might have enticed me any other time, knowing full well the influence this family had in the city of London at large, but as we were here on a more professional basis, I found it rather difficult to know how to carry myself. Was I in the superior position? Or the inferior?

Only time would tell, I supposed.

"Your mother said the deceased was her baby," Felix said. "I assume he was your youngest sibling?"

"Yes, he was," Miss Margaret said. She had luscious,

long hair the color of dark honey that rolled over her shoulders like a waterfall. "Younger than me by only a year."

"How old are you?" I asked. "Out of curiosity, honestly. Nothing more."

She swallowed, her jaw tight. "I am twenty-nine," she said.

I had not realized he was as young as that. Only a few years older than I, and he met the end that he did...

"Your brother was incredibly successful for as young as he was," Felix said. "From what we have heard, he had taken on many elaborate and extraordinary cases. Is that nothing more than an exaggeration, then?"

"No, not at all," Mr. Culpepper said, sitting down on the arm of his wife's chair, a delicate flower of a woman with tiny features in every regard and hair the color of spun silk. He looked a great deal more like his sister, with the same copper tones in his hair and the same sense of sharp dress. He also shared the same green eyes that it seemed every person in the family had. "He had been working as a barrister for the past...three years now? He completed easily two dozen cases in that time."

"Not two dozen," Mrs. Burke corrected him with a glare. "Come now, it couldn't have been more than fifteen, sixteen at most."

"I thought it was closer to thirty," Miss Margaret said.

It quickly turned into an argument between all the siblings, and I had to raise my hand into the air to draw the attention of both Mrs. Burke and Mr. Culpepper, who seemed to be the most at odds.

"My apologies," Mrs. Burke said, settling back against

her chair like an irritated squirrel who had been chased off by a bird. "That matters not, does it?"

"No, not particularly," I said. "We are interested more in his character as a person than we are about the amount of his work."

"His work was everything to him..." Miss Margaret said in a somewhat distant voice.

"What do you wish to know?" Mr. Culpepper asked.

I looked around at them all, my brow furrowing. "Well, if I may be so bold, I have noticed that apart from Miss Margaret, no one seems to be particularly concerned that their brother has died."

Felix's head snapped toward me, and I could feel his gaze burning into the side of my face, but I cared little for it. It was the truth and it was better for us all if we started with it.

"That's because we *aren't* terribly concerned," said Mr. Culpepper, folding his hands in his lap, shrugging his shoulders. "It must be confessed that Edward was an insufferable fellow."

Miss Margaret let out a small gasp, staring at her brother in horror. "Theodore..."

"Margaret, you must not pretend he was a saint," Mrs. Burke said with a roll of her large, green eyes in her sister's direction. "He was horrid, an utter fool, and you know it."

Miss Margaret's expression hardened and her bottom lip stuck out. She and my second cousin Marie had a great deal in common, I thought.

"He might have been a fool, but he was still our brother," she said. "How can you all be so unfeeling?"

"Margaret, I fear that you are only saddened because

Mother is so unhappy," Mr. Culpepper said. "Why, just a few days ago, you were saying how wretched and short-sighted he – "

Miss Margaret got to her feet, holding her hands out as if to stop an oncoming collision. "No, I will not hear it any longer. If you will please...excuse me."

She hurried from the room, but she didn't quite make it out the door before the sounds of her sobs reached us.

Mrs. Burke sighed heavily. "She is a sensitive thing..." she said.

Or she is right, and the rest of you are all far too unfeeling.

"He essentially ostracized us all," Mr. Culpepper said. "As the youngest, he was not to receive much of an inheritance, and as such, decided to go to law school on his own. As he studied, he worked at a law firm outside of Oxford, and there he took on the cases that no one else would. He only very recently became a full barrister in London, within the past nine months, I believe."

"That is correct," Mrs. Burke said. "He decided he was going to make his fortune in a way that Father would never expect, which was to only accept the sort of cases that would draw the attention of the newspapers and the wealthy."

"What sort of cases?" Felix asked. "Everyone keeps alluding to them, yet we have no examples."

"Oh, messy divorces, inheritance disputes, and lawsuits where people would attempt to sue businesses or family members," Mrs. Burke said. "While that all may not sound terribly exciting, it was the people he represented that were so colorful, and the situations they found themselves in that were so...ridiculous."

"For instance, one case he took on just about a year

ago was of a man who wished to leave his full inheritance to his cat," Mr. Culpepper said with a scoff. "Would you believe me if I told you that because of Edward, he was able to do that?"

"Or the time he represented a man who wished to marry a woman who was quite near to death," Mrs. Burke said. "Her family would not hear of it, but somehow, Edward managed to win the case, and they were married."

"The girl died two weeks later," Mr. Culpepper added. "And the now widowed husband had a hefty inheritance to make use of."

My brow furrowed. "It seems your brother had no scruples."

"No, not a one," Mr. Culpepper said. "We have not even told you of the case about the twins seeking alienation from one another – "

Mrs. Burke raised a hand. "No, Theodore. We do *not* need to revisit that case."

Felix shifted uncomfortably beside me, and I forced myself not to look at him. *Did she not want to tell us because we are twins? Or have they not quite realized that?*

"They certainly sound...interesting," Felix said, graciously.

"As to his death..." I said, wishing to quickly change the subject, not wanting to dwell on the idea of *twins* and *alienation*. "I assume that you here are all on the same page with Mrs. Burke as to how your brother died?" I asked.

As I looked around, it was clear that the general consensus was yes between them all. I saw a nod from

Mrs. Culpepper, and Mr. Burke said, "Yes, we do believe so."

"Her theory seems as sound as any others," Mr. Culpepper said. "How he died might be up for debate, but I have little doubt that he was murdered."

"How else could he have died, Theodore?" Mrs. Burke asked, acid eating away any remaining placidity in her tone. "We have been over this, with the timing and delivery of the drink – "

"Yes, yes, I understand," Mr. Culpepper said. "But is that not why we have brought them here? To find out what really happened? And why?"

He gestured toward Felix and I, and all eyes turned again to us.

"My theory is that he was poisoned as nothing more than a means of shutting him up," Mr. Burke said, his expression as sour as his wife's. "Someone might have seen it as doing the world a favor."

"Might I ask if there was anyone on this earth who actually liked your brother?" I asked. "Because if not, then it is going to be a difficult endeavor to discover exactly who took his life."

"Well, our mother, as you saw," Mr. Culpepper said.

"But even that is arguable," Mrs. Burke said. "They were always at odds. How many times did we hear her wailing about how wounded she was, and how he had broken her heart again and again?"

Mr. Culpepper rolled his eyes. "I suppose you are right. Apart from our mother, no. No one liked him."

"I assume he was not married?" Felix asked.

"No, not married," Mrs. Burke said.

"Was he seeing anyone?" I asked.

Mr. Culpepper and Mrs. Burke exchanged a questioning glance at one another across the room, but Mr. Culpepper shook his head. "No, not anymore he wasn't."

"The young woman he had been seeing most recently left him after their second time out together," Mrs. Burke said. "That was...perhaps two or three months ago, I cannot remember."

"She was a wise woman," Mr. Culpepper said.

The mention of a romance drew me back to the conversation I'd had with Gloria about a woman she knew that Mr. Edward Culpepper had also been in a relationship with. I wished I had asked her what the young woman's name was. "My cousin mentioned someone he had been seeing for quite some time, but she walked out on him because he did something to her that was...unforgivable?" I asked.

Mrs. Burke shook her head. "You are going to have to be more specific," she said.

"Yes, that could have been any of them," Mr. Culpepper said. "We have begun to lose count."

The butler appeared in the doorway, clapping the heels of his shoes together to alert us to his arrival. He bent himself into a bow. "My deepest apologies, but Lady Culpepper has asked that her children join her as the reverend has arrived for funeral plans. She says that it is most urgent."

Mrs. Burke sighed heavily, shaking her head. "Of all the times...fine, Fawkes, we are on our way. Tell her to hold herself together until we arrive, will you?"

He bowed again and ducked out of the room.

"I am sorry, Miss Crawford, but we must continue with the preparations," Mrs. Burke said. "I do hope that we have given you the information you needed, and answered your questions."

"I must admit there is still a great deal I do not know – " I said.

"If you need anything else, please do not hesitate to ask," Mrs. Burke said. "Goodbye, dear. Thank you for stopping by."

Before I could say anything more, we were being ushered away. Clearly, we would get no further information from anyone in this place.

6

_____

We pulled away from the estate no more than five minutes later, which did not trouble me too greatly as Lady Culpepper's wails could be heard filtering down through the corridors once again, likely at the presence of the reverend.

I let out a huff as we passed through the gates and back out onto the road again, heading north toward Richard's estate. "Well, that was disappointing," I said, brushing a loose strand of dark hair from my eyes. "What have we learned that we did not already come knowing?"

"We learned he was not married," Felix said, his eyes fixed outside at the world passing by us.

I glared at the side of his face. "Well, isn't that *so* incredibly helpful," I said. "At least we have eliminated the possibility his own wife was at her wit's end and decided to kill him."

Felix said nothing, simply continuing to stare out the window.

"How do they expect me to investigate this any

further when we were hardly there a quarter of an hour to learn about their brother?" I asked. "I realize the funeral needs preparing, but couldn't at least one of them have stayed with us to answer more questions about who might have wanted him dead?"

I shook my head, going over the conversation again in my mind.

"Then again, it seems that hardly anyone *liked* the man in the first place," I said. "That unfortunately leaves...well, everyone that knew him as a possible suspect."

Up in the front seat, our driver glanced at me in the rearview mirror, and I noticed his gaze shift quickly to Felix for a brief moment before turning to look back at the road.

"I don't even know where I might begin now," I said. "It could have been a client he refused to represent, or even the opposition of another case that went badly. It could have been any one of his family in that room, it could have been an old lover, a member of his household staff – "

Felix finally turned around to look at me, his Atlantic blue eyes piercing straight through me. "Lillian, I really don't think it is wise getting involved with this death," he said.

I snorted, arching my brow at him. "You cannot be serious," I said. "After all the trouble I have gone to, you are going to ask me to stop? Now?"

"I have been thinking on it, and this situation is entirely different than the two before it," he said. "In the first, you only decided to become involved when a killer attacked you in plain daylight, thinking the matter had become personal."

"That's true," I said. "That murderer on the ship orchestrated the whole thing rather well."

"And then with William's kidnapping, you wanted to find the killer of his caretaker because it involved our family, our cousin," Felix said.

"Right," I agreed.

"You are fiercely loyal, even to a fault," Felix said. "Blood is thicker than water, and all that, so it makes perfect sense to me why you would want to learn the truth about the other incidents. This time, though...why do you care?"

"I have already explained this to you," I said. "At length."

His eyes narrowed. "You have told me you want to do this because you can," he said. "To prove your skills to yourself or some such nonsense."

My mouth fell open. "Nonsense?" I asked. "Felix, you heard what Eugene said, that I have a unique ability that could prove useful to this family – "

Felix rolled his eyes. "Eugene Osbourn would say anything to make you think better of him," he said. "And do not try to pretend you really care one way or the other what the Culpepper family thinks of you. All you want is for them to publically praise you for doing your job well."

"What has gotten into you?" I asked. "Why the need for this attack on my character?"

"I'm not attacking you in any way," he said. "I am simply telling you the truth about – "

"What you are doing is throwing all of my flaws out into the open so that I may gaze upon them," I said. "Telling me I am vain and selfish – "

"You have no reason, no *real* reason, to be investing yourself in such dangerous things," Felix said, his face screwing up in frustration. "What good could possibly come of immersing yourself in the death of a stranger? And not just a death, but a murder? What good, Lillian?"

"This isn't only about finding the person that killed him," I said. "This is more than just to prove to myself that I can – "

"Very well, then the reason you want to prove it is so you may write home to Mother and Father, as nothing more than a means of upsetting them," he said. "You have been trying to make them regret ever sending us out here."

I stared at him, the anger simmering just beneath the surface. "Are you quite through?" I asked, my eyes flashing.

"You are acting like an utter fool, Lillian, going so far out of your way to have your revenge on Mother and Father," Felix said. "Why could you not be happy with simply enjoying the time we have here with our cousins, and living our life in a quiet, uneventful manner – "

"Your first mistake is to assume the only reason I am doing this is to get back at Mother and Father," I hissed through my teeth. "Certainly, I am pleased that I am succeeding where they expected me to fail. They were wrong about me, and wrong about you, too. You cannot fault me for wanting to take charge of the situation and right my reputation."

Felix said nothing, simply continuing to stare coolly at me.

"If I remember correctly, you and I *both* were very happy to be away from home, so that we might make a new name for ourselves, away from our pasts, away from all the mistakes we had made. This was to be our fresh start, wasn't it?" I asked.

"And you have chosen to become some sort of detective, like a heroine in a novel, investigating murders?" Felix asked. "Do you not understand how ridiculous it sounds?"

"Why is it so strange?" I asked. "I am good at it. I have the stomach for it. And, to be perfectly honest, I find great satisfaction in doing something like this...something that *matters*."

"Who *else* do you know that does anything remotely as dark as this?" Felix asked. "Honestly, of all the occupations with which you could employ yourself, you choose to put yourself in danger, chasing after killers, snooping around in secret, lying and deceiving – "

"You didn't seem to mind the other times I have done this. Why are you only just voicing your objections now?" I asked.

"I made it quite clear I didn't think you should continue with this after Mrs. Burke left the first time," Felix said. "If I had known she was coming, I would have made it clear beforehand, and advised you not to see her."

"I have already agreed to do this," I said, folding my arms. "I've made up my mind."

"You are not going to reconsider?" he asked.

"Why would I?" I asked. "Mrs. Burke said she had heard of my success and knew that I would be especially suited to find her brother's killer."

"She should have taken it to the police," Felix said. "Insisted they look into it."

"She tried and they didn't believe her. Anyway, I know that I can solve this for her," I said.

"How?" Felix asked, incredulous. "Did you not just say that you have no idea where to begin?"

"Well, there is that lover the victim had taken that Gloria mentioned," I said. "I intend to begin there, and see if she can point me in a useful direction."

"And if that leads nowhere?" he asked.

"Then I will figure out what to do when I get there," I said, glaring at him. "Look, if you are so upset about my decision, you do not have to continue on with me. If you want to duck out, you can."

He sat up a bit straighter in his seat, adjusting the front of his coat. "Very well," he said in a low voice. "That is what I am going to do, then."

I gaped at him. His answer was not at all what I had expected.

It was not long before we pulled into the drive of the estate, and neither of us had spoken for almost half an hour. Stiff as a piece of cold steel, I stared out the window, my body trembling with anger. Everything I wanted to say to Felix battered against the inside of my head, but I could not find the strength to say any of it, the good or the ugly.

We'd had our share of quarrels in the past, some of which had ended at hair-raising volumes that required the intervention of our parents. Just as many were nothing more than short spats which quickly ended when one of us needed the other.

This, however...somehow, this felt different. I didn't think I had ever been this angry at him, nor felt so divided from him. I knew him better than I knew myself.

How could we allow something to drive such a wedge between us?

Even so, I could not swallow my pride. I refused to throw this chance away, even if he thought I should. What of what I wanted? I knew full well that he was simply trying to protect me, but did he not see the potential? Did he not realize that he didn't need to protect me like he was trying to?

A small, nagging voice at the back of my mind contradicted each of those thoughts, in Felix's voice, no less, but the molten magma of my anger sloshed overtop of it all, smothering the arguments.

We pulled up to the front of the house, and Felix hardly waited for the car to come to a complete stop before he swung the door open and stepped out.

I slid out as well, but laid my hand on the open window of Ronald, the chauffeur's, door. "Wait one moment, Ronald. I would like for you to take me somewhere else in just a few minutes, but I must go inside and get something, first."

Felix turned around at that, sliding his hands into his pockets, gazing at me with an expression that gave nothing away, but his eyes filled with frustration. "Where are you going now?" he asked.

"Well, if you aren't going to help me, then I am going to ask someone else to step in for you," I said, folding my arms. "I am going to see Eugene."

Felix's face hardened, but he quickly smoothed it over, giving me a small shrug with only one shoulder. He started to turn away again, sending my blood boiling through my body, my chest tingling with the frustration.

"You are making your decision, Felix," I called after

him, my nails digging into the flesh of my arms. "And I am making mine."

He gave me a wave over his shoulder, and continued on up the steps without another look back.

I found myself still standing there, staring after him, long after he'd disappeared through the doors.

"Ah...Miss Crawford?" the driver asked. "Was that Mr. Osbourn you were talking about? Me taking you there, that is?"

"Yes," I said. "Unless Richard has somewhere else for you to be?"

"No, it should be all right," he said with a nervous grin. "If you would allow me just a moment to let him know where I'll be. Shouldn't be more than a minute or two, if you wait here for me."

"I will meet you here," I answered. "As I said, I have someone to speak with, too."

I followed Felix's footsteps up the stairs, my heart hammering in my chest, worrying if he might be waiting to give me yet another lecture as soon as I stepped inside the house. He was nowhere to be found, however, which gave me clearance to start up the stairs to my destination.

I felt strangely exposed as I walked up the winding staircase alone, so used to the familiar presence of Felix at my side, especially since coming to England.

Perhaps I have begun to rely on him too much. This could be good for me. I need to find a way to stand on my own two feet, don't I? I can't always have him holding me back with his fears and his troubles.

This was about more than just the argument we'd had in the car, I knew. This whole unease between the two of us stemmed from his confession about his supposed guilt in Daniel's drowning...something I was still uncertain whether I believed or not.

He started all this. If he had only kept his mouth shut about the whole matter, allowed it to remain in the past where we had already dealt with it...but, no! For some reason, he feels the need to drag it all back out into the light and stare at it, readdress it... Why does he want my pity? Why does he insist on victimizing himself?

I rounded the corner at the top of the stairs, making my way past William's room. His door was closed, which meant he had likely gone out into the garden to play. I did not stop until I reached the second to last door on the right, and raised my hand to knock.

"Who is it?" came Gloria's voice.

"Lillian," I said. "I need to speak with you for a moment."

There was no response.

"Please."

"What could you possibly have to say to me?" she snapped. "Go away."

I clenched my jaw, the anger barely having a chance to cool at all on my walk up, and it now rumbled to the surface once again, threatening to boil over. "You mentioned that friend of yours yesterday, the friend who had been courted by Mr. Culpepper?" I asked anyway, ignoring her request. Perhaps a bit of drama would pique her curiosity. "I was hoping that you would – "

"I said go away, didn't I?" she shouted through the door.

I tried to refrain, but the molten rage pushed me over the edge. I flung the door open, striding in.

Gloria lay stretched out on her belly across a fainting

couch in the corner of her room, an open book lying in front of her. She gaped at me as I looked around.

"Glad to see that I am not interrupting anything important," I said, glaring at her. "Now, tell me the girl's name."

"I did not give you permission to come in here," she said, sitting up, her eyes the narrow slits they always seemed to become when I was around. "Yet here you are, doing as you please, just as you always do."

"Oh, save it for someone who cares," I said. "I came for your help, humbly might I add, and you simply refused to – "

"Humble is not at all the word I would use to describe any of your actions, cousin," she said, slowly getting to her feet. "So why do you expect me to do as you ask, despite your complete disregard for my wishes?"

"I came to you with a simple question, a question that you could have answered so much more quickly than engaging in this silly argument!" I snapped. "It would have taken you no longer than a minute to give me the name of your friend, and where I might find her. That is all I want, and if you give me that information, I will leave you alone."

Gloria stared at me, seemingly stunned.

"Fine," she said. "Her name is Virtue Bellingham, and she sings some nights down at the *Mare and Magnolia* outside London. Now, get out!" she cried as she came toward me, grabbing me by the arm, and shoving me back out through the door.

She slammed the door in my face, sending some of my dark hair flying away from my head.

I blinked at the door, stunned myself at my hasty departure. I had not expected that of her. Not at all.

Not all dogs are all bark and no bite, it seems.

Fuming, I balled my hands into fists and started back down the hall, heading toward the car.

"It seems everyone in this house is beginning to despise me..." I muttered under my breath. It wouldn't be long before Marie found some reason to, and Richard.

I supposed the only person whose good graces I might remain in was William. *He* would understand why I was doing what I was doing, why I wanted to solve this murder.

Who am I kidding? The boy hardly knows anything about what really happened when he was kidnapped. His father won't even tell him that his caretaker died as a result of trying to save him!

"I don't need them...not any of them," I murmured, stepping back out into the grey, dull afternoon. "And I suppose none of them need me, either."

"Are you ready to go, Miss?" the chauffeur asked from where he stood beside the car.

"Yes, Ronald," I said through tight lips, allowing him to open the door for me. "And let us not delay a moment longer."

7

"What a pleasant surprise!"

I might have enjoyed the introduction to the Osbourn family estate if it were not for the sorry state in which I found myself. The whole ride over left me seething, my mind filled with all of the things I might have said that would have, perhaps, been better responses to Felix's concerns and questions, which made me all the angrier. I chewed over the frustration, the rage, the deep hurt I felt. He had slighted me, seemingly without thought, and walked away from me knowing full well what it would mean.

He made that decision to walk away. Not me.

"You do not have to lie," I said now, making my way across the terrace to where Eugene Osbourn stood to greet me. "I know full well that I have shown up entirely unannounced, and how that must make me look."

"Spontaneous, I would say," Eugene said with a smile, but as he studied my face more closely, his expression slipped a little. "Something is the matter, I take it? Something to do with your investigation?"

"You might say that..." I said, looking around. "It seems I interrupted some quiet contemplation?"

The chair he'd been sitting in had been pulled away from the others, nestled beneath the shade of an elm tree whose branches stretched over the terrace itself. A half finished cup of tea sat on the slate stone beside the leg of the chair, along with the book he'd closed upon my arrival.

"A bit of an evening ritual," he said. "After dinner, I often enjoy some time away from the rest of the family. Honestly, it began as my personal time to grieve the loss of my sister...but has since come to a place where I might regain some peace of mind as I pursue the task of study."

"Study?" I asked, bending down to retrieve the book. "Ah, I see. Spurgeon."

"Yes, a brilliant man with great wisdom," he said as I turned the book over in my hands. "He speaks truth in a way that I understand; direct, believing that what he had to say was far more important than taking care to preserve the feelings of those who heard him." He smirked at me. "Much like someone else I know."

Despite my frustrations, my cheeks burned ever so slightly. "A flaw, some might say."

"I, on the other hand, find it refreshing," he said. "You and I live in a world where everyone says one thing, but means something entirely different. You, though...I never have to wonder if you are telling me the truth. I always know you don't see the need to mask your true thoughts."

I shrugged. "There is little sense in it, even if it has gotten me into trouble."

"Here, come sit down with me," he said, gesturing down the steps to a gazebo surrounded by rose bushes in full bloom. "We will not be disturbed or overheard down here."

He held his hand out to me, which gave me pause for a brief moment.

I quickly realized I didn't need to be angry with him as I was with Felix. He was *not* Felix. I could relax around him.

He and I sat down together on the bench seat that wrapped all the way around the inside of the gazebo, the heady scent of the roses drifting in on the warm, evening breeze. It surprised me how...romantic it felt, despite the fact that I had come to discuss an investigation about murder with him.

"Well, then..." he said. "What is it that you wished to speak with me about?"

I said, "I hoped you would be willing to help me with part of my investigation."

"I would be happy to assist in any way I can," he said, his brow furrowing slightly. "I assume Felix is taking care of matters elsewhere?"

"No," I said. "He and I had a ridiculous quarrel earlier today over the whole thing."

"I see," he said. "Are you all right?"

"Oh, I am perfectly fine," I said, folding my arms. "I know I am in the right. He was completely out of line. He made me seem like a fool."

"Did you wish to talk about it?" he asked.

"No," I said flatly. "No, I do not."

"Very well," Eugene said. "It would not be my place to get involved, anyway."

"He and I happen to see this whole situation in two entirely different ways," I said, despite not wanting to delve into it. The words just seemed to spew from my mouth. "He doesn't want me to pursue it, and I have chosen to. He disagrees heartily with that, and as such, he has decided he does not want to help me."

"Oh," Eugene said, his brow furrowing.

I looked at him. "Which is why I have come to you for assistance," I said. "You were the first person I thought of who might be able to help."

Eugene frowned, rubbing his hand over his jaw. "Felix didn't seem keen on you working on this investigation when I was there yesterday, either," he said. "What was his reasoning?"

"He said the other two times I have done any kind of investigating, it has been a personal matter," I said. "This time, the victim is a complete stranger."

"That doesn't seem to be a terribly strong argument," Eugene said.

"He also is concerned about my safety, saying I am needlessly throwing myself into dangerous situations," I said.

"Well, it has been a miracle you have walked away from previous incidents with your life, I will give him that," Eugene said.

I glared at him. "That isn't even the real root of his problem, though..." I drummed my fingers against my arms, wondering if I should even voice it. The ugliness of it dug at me, deeply, and made my stomach sick. "He thinks the only reason I am really pursuing any of this is to have some sort of revenge against our parents for sending us all the way out here to stay with our cousins."

"Revenge?" Eugene asked. "As if coming to London was some sort of punishment for you?"

"That's precisely what they hoped it would be," I snapped. "What they didn't seem to realize, however, is that they removed both Felix and I from the lives and the pasts that we were all too happy to leave behind. In the end, they really were only doing us a favor."

He studied me, his gaze scrutinizing. "Your past, huh...?"

I frowned. I had said too much. "Who doesn't have some things they would rather leave behind?" I asked. "My point is, he is wrong about why I want to do this."

"Why do you want to?" Eugene asked. "It is something I have wondered, myself."

"Because I know I can!" I said. "You even said it yourself, I have a talent for this. Not just anyone can sift through the lies of others, pick up on the subtle nuances of body language, recognize connections between people... I have those skills. And, it seems, a strong enough stomach to be able to face some of the less than savory parts of these investigations."

"Yes, and that is curious, isn't it?" Eugene said. "It's something I've wondered as well...how do you deal with it?"

I looked away. "I've seen the ugliness of people," I said. "I can see that most people hate one another so much they wish they were dead. It seems that I have finally stepped into the realm where people have actually gone through with it."

"It doesn't surprise you, these deaths?" he asked.

I shook my head. "No, not really. People kill out of passion. Passion comes in two forms, and they can both lead to obsession, which then leads to self-destruction," I said. "The deepest infatuations...and the deepest hatreds."

"I suppose I never thought of those two as similar," Eugene said. "I always put them on opposite ends of the spectrum."

"Love is not passion," I said. "Love is choice. There is a great difference. Love can *have* passion, of course. But when someone takes a lover, whether for good or for ill, what happens at the onset? All those feelings, rushing to your head, clogging up your thoughts. Hatred is much the same. The surge of emotions floods like a torrent, making it difficult to think of anything else. You can lose sleep, lose any desire to eat. All you can think about is that person."

"I suppose you are right..." he said.

"I see through people's lies," I said. "It is no special gift, just years of spending time with these sorts of people, just as you said. Perhaps I am uniquely able to do this, but if I can, and if I want to simply because I – well, I don't know if I could confidently say that I *enjoy* it – but I am good at it. What is so wrong with that?"

"Perhaps you have been uniquely gifted for this task," Eugene said. "Equipped, prepared..."

"And do not think that it is lost on me what you said before," I continued, my voice lowering. "You are good to remind me that I would be helping people by doing this."

He smiled at me. "And you certainly would be."

I sighed. "This Culpepper family, however... I think all they are hoping to find is the truth. There are many who do not need closure about the victim's death. From what I have learned, he was not terribly well liked. It seems that no one apart from his mother and perhaps one of his sisters cares that he is gone."

"Well, then see this as a way of honing your skills," he said. "Your first real go at the endeavor. Who knows? You might find you change your mind, or solidify your resolve."

"You're right," I said. "If I do like it, then maybe I should set up shop as a private investigator or some such, give people the chance to come and hire me."

I looked out over the garden, the sun just dipping below the tree line.

"Are you certain you wish to help me?" I asked. "I know it might make people question you, given your sterling reputation."

"Yes, of course I'm certain," Eugene said. "I think it would be very beneficial for me to help. I realize that Culpepper's death occurring at my concert is no responsibility of mine, but this could be a way for me to help the family regardless. It does not sit well with me that I have done nothing apart from offer a letter of condolence."

"Well, I am glad to have your assistance," I said. "Which happens to be something I am in need of this evening."

"Oh? And what exactly do you need of me?" he asked.

"I am heading to a jazz club on the outskirts of the city," I said. "And I know it would appear rather strange for me to go there unaccompanied."

"Of course," he said. "I am happy to join you. Allow me the chance to inform my uncle that we are going to be taking the car into town, and then you can fill me in on all the details on our way."

I did just that as we drove toward the club, which

Eugene's cousin had happened to know. After some gentle guidance about proper attire, we set out into the darkening evening.

The location of the club was unassuming as we approached. It brought us just beside what looked to be an abandoned warehouse of some sort, and it wasn't until we stepped out of the car that we could hear the pulse of the music from somewhere nearby.

The street itself surely would have seemed dead during the day, but at night, it seemed every window in the shops and restaurants the whole way up and down shone brightly. People strolled in and out of doors, all elaborately dressed in the latest fashions. Streetlamps glowed between some of the shops.

"My cousin did warn us that it was Saturday evening," Eugene said. "Always a crowded time. Come on, the door to the club is right over here," he added, offering his arm to me.

We walked up the stairs, and found ourselves standing face to face with a man who wore a dark suit, hat, and gloves, blending him into the shadowy entryway. "Sorry. 'Less you have an invitation, you aren't welcome."

"An invitation?" Eugene asked, looking down at me.

I frowned. Gloria had not mentioned the place was invitation only.

"Yeah," the burly man responded. "So if you don' have one, you can jus' get lost."

"I'm sorry," Eugene said, laying a hand gracefully over his heart. "I suppose you do not recognize me. My name is Eugene Osbourn, the concert pianist?"

The burly man only stared at him, his expression blank.

"I am quite certain that if you were to check with whomever it is that owns this club, they would make an exception for me and my guest," Eugene said, his voice taking on a steely edge that I had never heard before. His kind smile, too, seemed a bit twisted.

The guard at the door pursed his lips and turned away. "Give me a moment," he said, and disappeared inside.

I looked up at Eugene and smirked. "My, my. I didn't realize you had such arrogance in you."

He looked nervous, but smiled. "Well, what good is my reputation if I can't throw it around once in a while? For the overall good of the investigation, that is."

"Right, for the investigation," I said, my smile growing. "I must admit I am rather impressed."

It was dark, and so difficult to tell, but I thought I saw the smallest hint of pride flicker in his eyes.

The employee returned, and cleared his throat. "My deepest apologies, sir. You were not expected, but are o' course welcome." He pulled the door open, and stood aside to let us pass.

I grinned. "Thank you, kind sir," I said, taking Eugene's arm once more.

The man nodded, seemingly not too put out by the whole affair, and closed the door behind us.

Eugene squeezed my hand tucked into the crook of his arm with his own, and a jolt shot through my arm from the point he touched me. Why did I find myself enjoying it so much?

You are not here for fun. This is for the investigation.

But seeing the heart of the club as we came out of the

narrow, dark tunnel made me wish we were there for the merriment of it.

The room, though easily three stories tall, seemed intimate as thick, red, velvety curtains lined the walls, blocking out all the windows. Round tables dotted the room, draped in more rich, red linens and silks, and the only lights apart from small lamps on each table were directed at the stage where a woman stood at a silver standing microphone.

She wore a dress of golden silk, which matched the starburst pin in her hair that reminded me of a firework cracking against the blackness of the night sky that was her hair. She crooned into the microphone, cradling it between her hands. She had accompaniment from a saxophone, a cellist, and a piano player.

"Ah, Mr. Osbourn, I had hoped to find you," said a nervous voice beside us.

A wiry man with wild curls atop his head approached us.

"I am the owner of this establishment," he said. "Mr. Oliver Swede."

"Good evening, Mr. Swede," Eugene said. "And thank you for your kindness at allowing us entry last minute like this."

"Of course, of course," the man said, dabbing at his forehead with a handkerchief. "I – I always leave a prime table available for prestigious clientele who might just want to – to stop by." He giggled nervously and gestured toward an empty table nearer the stage. "If you would follow me..."

"Of course," Eugene said.

We followed the man as he wound his way between

the tables where couples sat together in quiet adoration of the music and one another, most of them entirely oblivious to us as we passed by.

"Now, might I offer you something to drink? We have everything you can think of, sir, anything your heart desires. I employ some of the best bartenders around, and would be happy to fetch whatever you want."

"Thank you," Eugene said. "I'm afraid that I cannot stay terribly long, but for now would be happy to have a tonic water."

"A...tonic water?" Mr. Swede asked, his face paling. "Are you quite certain, sir?"

"Yes," Eugene said. "I have a performance practice tomorrow, and do not wish to dampen the senses."

"Oh, of course, yes, I understand," Mr. Swede said, but his expression made it perfectly clear he was lying. "I shall fetch you a – tonic water, yes. And for the lady?"

"Would you by any chance happen to have some coffee?" I asked.

"Ah, another American," Mr. Swede said. "Yes, we certainly do. I hope that a pot made fresh from beans shipped straight from the Caribbean will be sufficient?"

"That sounds fine," I said, knowing full well that most of the coffee I drank back in New York came from there. "I prefer Italian, but I suppose that will do."

Mr. Swede's smile fell, and he dipped his head, his wiry, pale hair bouncing. "Right away. I shall have them sent to you right – right away."

"Wait, before you go," Eugene said. He nodded toward the woman singing on the low stage. "Is that woman Miss Virtue Bellingham?"

"Oh, yes," Mr. Swede said. "She is our most popular

singer. Everyone requests her performances. I always do well when she is here."

"I imagine she is quite popular with the gentlemen?" Eugene asked.

Mr. Swede's eyes widened. "Oh, I – I assumed that you came with this lovely young lady," he said, laughing in his nervous way. "If you would care for an introduction, I would be happy to arrange it after she is finished this evening."

"You misunderstand me," Eugene began.

"She is a friend of my cousin," I interrupted, leaning across Eugene's arm to look at Mr. Swede. "I am hoping to speak with her about something important."

Mr. Swede's face fell. "Oh, um...yes, of course. I can arrange that. She is very busy, you know. I cannot have you taking up much of her time."

"It won't take more than a few minutes," I said, giving him as sweet a smile as I could muster.

"Very well, then I shall go and order your – your coffee, yes? And your tonic water. Please, enjoy your evening."

He turned and scurried away, leaving us in peace.

I snorted, leaning closer to Eugene just as he let out a low chuckle as well.

"My goodness," I whispered. "The poor man. All excited to have our business and then we disappoint him."

"I feel rather bad about it," Eugene murmured, but still smiled, leaning close enough for me to feel his breath against my ear. "He is doing his best to accommodate us, and at the last minute."

"Yes, I guess he is," I said. "Still, he seemed to be torn

between bullying us into spending more money or fawning over you."

"Yes, well...at least he isn't suspicious of our real reasons for wanting to speak with her, or he might not let us near her," Eugene said. He gave me a sidelong look. "And you like Italian coffee, hmm? Remind me to have my uncle's cook brew you a real pot, the next time you are visiting."

I smiled at him. "I would like that, I think."

The song came to a crescendo, and the small crowd in the room began to applaud the singer and the players.

Eugene and I joined in, him more enthusiastically than me.

"That was *Dance of a Thousand Dances,*" he said in a low voice as the next song began. "And, if I'm not mistaken, this one is called *Mystic Moon.*"

"Your knowledge of music is impressive," I said in a whisper. "Though I suppose I should expect nothing less of one of the world's most famous pianists."

"You give me more credit than I'm due," he said. "I learned many of the pieces I learned just by hearing them and practicing them myself. I suppose in a way, I had to work harder and pay closer attention as one of my senses was absent at the time. I couldn't read the piece and allow it to flow that way. I had to memorize it."

My eyes widened. "I suppose I never realized all that music you know is memorized. That's incredible. Even now, with your sight returned?"

"Even now, it is how I prefer to practice," he said. "I have grown accustomed to that style of learning the music and I prefer it. Here...why don't you close your eyes, and just *listen* to the music? See how your mind creates its own images to correspond to it, and how you simply feel it more."

"Close my eyes? Right now?" I asked, glancing briefly up at the stage.

"We have some time to pass," he said. "The girl we have come to question is in the middle of her performance. We won't be able to question her until the show is over."

"True," I said.

"Go on, give it a try," he said. "Just for a moment. Give yourself the chance to see as I did for so many years."

I felt foolish, but he was right that we had little else to do with the time.

I closed my eyes, and at once became worried about my surroundings. My eyelids flew open and I blinked, looking around.

"It's all right," he murmured. "Just pay attention to the music. I'll keep an eye on everything."

I knew he would, and so, I did as he asked, and closed my eyes again.

It wasn't as if I was a stranger to closing my eyes. It happened all the time. However, I could not remember the last time I closed my eyes with the intention of depriving myself of my sense of sight. Colors and light still filtered through my eyelids, but the rest of my senses seemed to elevate. I caught a whiff of bergamot as someone's footsteps passed by our table. I heard the shift of ice in a drink behind me, clinking against the side of the glass. The soft feel of Eugene's shift brushed against my arm beside me.

And the music...it seemed deeper, richer as I paid close attention to it. I could hear the cello more clearly, the change in each note of the saxophone. I listened to the woman's voice, clear as a bird song, singing of a lost love. The shift of the piano keys struck me, not following the rhythm of the song exactly as I might have expected. A bit of improvisation.

"It's...different," I murmured. "Fuller, if that's possible."

I opened my eyes and found him gazing at me. His face slipped into a warm smile as my eyes adjusted to the dark room once again.

"You are quite lovely when you let your guard down," he said, a quiet softness in his voice.

My cheeks flushed. I felt rather stunned, and vulnerable. I *had* let my guard down...hadn't I?

He held his hand out to me. "Would you care to dance?" he asked.

It seemed surreal, the whole affair. Perhaps it was the darkness of the room, or the lull of the piano. Maybe it was the guise that we were there in a somewhat undercover capacity. Either way, for a moment, things felt...different.

I laid my hand in his. What could the harm be in a dance? Although Cousin Richard had once accused me of knowing no dances but the Charleston and Foxtrot, I was actually practiced in all types of dancing.

"I should warn you," I said as he pulled me to my feet. "I have taken classes with some of New York's best dance instructors. I have yet to find a partner who does not step on my feet."

"Well, then prepare to be surprised..." he said.

He immediately spun me into a twirl, with grace and an effortlessness that was unlike anything I had experienced in all my years attending parties and balls. It was as if he was anticipating my movements, more aware of them than even the most skilled partners I had the pleasure of dancing with. He was...good. Better than good.

His arm wrapped around my waist, and we began to dance more closely as the song changed again to a lulling melody. We smiled at one another.

Strangely, for a moment I could imagine the two of us dancing just this way many months, even perhaps years from now. We could look back on this night and think of how wonderful it was, how romantic.

Thomas Williams certainly never took me out dancing like this. We never did anything that I might have enjoyed, but I had never stopped to think that it was odd. I had fawned over Thomas for so long that when he had chosen me, I knew I would have followed him anywhere. Broken free of that accursed blindness that only infatuation could cause, I now saw him for the selfish swine he really had been.

"You are a marvelous dancer," Eugene murmured, and his words tickled my ear.

"Thank you," I said. "I studied it for many years."

"As did I," he said. "Music seems to draw me in any way that it can."

I smirked. "Well, I have certainly danced with worse partners."

"My, that is a compliment, coming from you," he said. "For I know you must have attended countless engagements where you would have been expected to dance."

"That is true," I said. "And I've danced with so many partners that I've lost count."

"Well, I hope I am able to do you proud with my skill."

I leaned in a bit closer, and his hand wrapped more tightly around me.

It felt...all right. It felt good to be this close. Safe. Comfortable. There were no pretenses, no awkward conversation. We could just enjoy the dance and the company of each other.

I looked up at him, and he smiled down at me.

Our dancing slowed, his smile shifting into an expression of...what? It was difficult to explain, but I could *feel* his focus sharpening, narrowing in on me, and me alone.

My heart began to race.

The song came to a dramatic close, and applause erupted around the room.

With a jolt, I leaned away from Eugene and looked around, finding some of the guests on their feet, giving the musicians a standing ovation.

I glared at the interruption. *It isn't as if we are at some grand theater, you fools.*

Lights pointing at the small stage grew suddenly in brightness, and some of the veiled romance in the room dissipated as the imperfections became more apparent.

"Well..." Eugene said, slowly – perhaps a bit too slowly – removing his arms from around me. "I suppose now would be the best time to talk to Miss Bellingham, would it not?"

"Right, of course," I said, quickly checking my hair, sweeping some feathered pieces from my eyesight. "Let's go, then. No sense in wasting any more time."

I strode over to the stage, keeping my face turned

away from him. I didn't want him to see the deep flush in my cheeks now that the lights had come fully on.

The woman seemed younger than she had from a distance, as we approached. She could not have been much older than I was. She was a pretty thing, for sure. Even beautiful. I could see why the late Mr. Culpepper might have come here again and again to see her, and eventually to ask her to dinner. Perhaps her singing bewitched him. If not, then her bright, wide smile certainly would have.

"Good evening," I said, striding right up onto the stage, despite the strange looks I was receiving from the cellist who was busy settling his instrument into its case. "Are you Miss Virtue Bellingham?" I asked.

"Yes, I am," she said brightly, though sounding somewhat out of breath. "It is always a pleasure to meet an admirer of my singing."

I shook my head. "Yes, you were very good, but that isn't why I am here," I said. "I had hoped to ask you a few questions about – "

Her face fell, and some of the color drained from her cheeks. "Is this about Mr. Culpepper?" she asked.

"Yes, I – " I said.

She shook her head, starting to walk backwards away from me, her hands held up before her, as if to ward me off. "No, no. I don't want to answer any questions. Yes, I knew him. Yes, we were seeing one another at one point. But no, I have no idea what happened to him."

8

M y eyes narrowed, and I took a few steps after her. *Have the police already been by to talk to her?* If they had been, then it seemed that they had lied to Mrs. Burke, or Mrs. Burke had lied to me.

I was about to open my mouth to ask this precise question when Eugene stepped up beside me.

"Your performance was marvelous," Eugene said, inclining his head to the girl. "Our apologies for spooking you like this."

I glanced up at him, and at once, I saw Felix standing beside me, doing the very same; smoothing the conversation over, the gentleness to my sharp attack. Pride prevented me from taking any personal blame for the matter, knowing full well that I probably should have.

"Thank – Thank you," the young woman said, her rich brown eyes turning up to Eugene as he appeared. "Are you Mr. Osbourn? The famous pianist?"

Eugene's face split into an embarrassed smile. "Yes..." he said. "I am surprised you recognized me."

"I – I can hardly believe this!" the girl exclaimed, her hands knitting tightly together as she practically trembled with excitement. "I have been to three of your performances! I have listened to many of your pieces. I can't believe I am meeting you, here, now!"

A twinge of annoyance bubbled up within me, and I folded my arms, looking up at Eugene.

"You are too kind," he said. "You have a voice like an angel, but I am sure you have heard that many times."

"Not from someone like you!" she exclaimed.

"The way you sang *Mystic Moon*... I have never heard anyone else – "

"Yes, yes, it was all lovely," I interrupted. "We have come for a reason, Miss Bellingham."

"Right, of course," Eugene said, clearing his throat. "I suppose you must have thought we were with the police, didn't you?"

The girl's eyes widened again, but she seemed less frightened now. "Yes, I did..." she said. "I have been waiting for them to show up any day now."

"Well, we are not the police, nor are we working with them," I said. "We have been hired by Mr. Culpepper's family to look into his death."

Her eyes shifted back and forth from Eugene and I. "His family? Do they think – do they think I had something to do with it?"

"That's why we are here," I said. "To speak with you."

"We would just like to talk," Eugene said. "Ask a few questions about him, and those he might have been connected with. Perhaps you would be able to direct us toward someone who would have wanted to hurt Mr. Culpepper or who had a reason to have him removed?"

The girl's jaw clenched, and she swallowed hard.

I then saw the need to offer an olive branch. "Look, we are well aware of Mr. Culpepper's poor reputation," I said. "Even to his family, he was not very well-liked. We know the list of those who *did* like him is much, much shorter than the list of those who had a bone to pick with him."

She folded her arms, and looked back and forth, eyeing the other musicians who were quite obviously lingering to hear what we were all talking about.

She leaned in close, her voice dropping to a whisper. "Not here. Follow me."

She started off the stage, and with nothing more than a glance between us, Eugene and I went after her.

We followed her between the low, round tables to the back, where she disappeared behind one of the velvet drapes. Beyond we found a long hall, dimly lit and smelling of mildew. All the doors remained closed, apart from the one she opened at the end.

A dressing room greeted us, clean and sparse, with nothing more than a floor-length mirror and a trunk beneath the window. A collection of makeup and brushes sat on the windowsill, which overlooked part of the busy, colorful street below.

"Close the door," she told Eugene as we came into the room behind her.

Eugene obliged, and then turned back to her.

"I will have you know..." the girl said, reaching toward her sleeve. "I do have the means of protecting myself. I might not be able to take you both out, but I would be able to do some damage before – "

"We aren't here to harm you," I said, not bothering to

mention the pair of knives that I carried with me tucked inside my garter. "If you really were worried about that, then you never should have let us follow you back here."

She didn't seem to have an answer to that thought.

"Miss Bellingham, if I may..." Eugene said, stepping up. "We realize that this whole affair must have upset you a great deal, otherwise you would not have had the answers at the ready the way you did when we approached you. It was as if you have been rehearsing them."

"I suppose, in a way, I have been," she said, striding to the windowsill. One by one, she began to pull pins from her hair, scattering them into a green glass bowl reflecting the light of the moon above. "I heard just this morning that he had died, and immediately I began to worry that my relationship with him might come back to light. I worried that someone might come and ask me about it, as strange as his death seemed to be, or might try to offer me their condolences if they thought we were still in said relationship... I didn't want either."

"Why would someone come and ask you about his death?" I asked. "Do you think anyone might have thought you were involved in it?"

"That's what I didn't know," she said. "Our acquaintance ended poorly. Anyone that knows him or I knows that."

"What happened?" Eugene asked. "If you do not mind me asking."

She sighed, and turned away. She picked up a brush and began running it through her thick, dark hair as she stepped in front of the mirror. "Well, it's a bit of a tale. He came to the club one night when I was singing, and asked the manager to meet with me afterward. He was... charming and smooth. I hate to even admit that I found his wiles attractive at any point in time. He kept coming to the club after that, always when I was performing. Eventually, he asked me if I would be interested in dinner with him, in going dancing with him..."

Her eyebrows furrowed at her reflection as she tugged as some difficult curls near the back of her head. "I never thought I could be so lucky. A girl like me catching the eye of such a man. A wealthy barrister, no less. It seemed terribly romantic..." She shook her head, slamming her brush back down onto the windowsill.

I glanced over at Eugene, my eyebrows high. It was clear she despised her past self for her thoughtless falling head over heels for the man. The dislike, as strong as it was, might just be the motivation for murder that we were looking for.

I smirked at him, and he smiled back. *Well, well... maybe we managed to hit the target straight on this time. Think of how the family will praise me for finding the culprit so soon.*

"We saw each other briefly but what I thought was exclusively," she went on, grabbing a fringed silk shawl of jade green from her trunk and throwing it over her shoulders. "One night when we were having a very intimate dinner at one of London's finest establishments...I told him that I was in love with him."

I stared at her hardening expression in the mirror. There was hatred...I could see it, like the flash of cold steel.

A nasty, mirthless smile spread across her face as she twisted her hair up behind her head into a tight knot, twirling it around with the point of her finger. "Do you know what he did?" she asked, a slight hitch in her last words. She lowered her hands, and stared at herself, blankly. "He laughed at me."

"Laughed?" I asked. "Because of your admission?"

She turned around and nodded. "Yes. He wiped his face with his napkin, thanked me for all the fun we'd had, got up from the table...and walked out."

"How cruel," Eugene said.

"He had no heart, plain and simple," Miss Bellingham snapped, drawing her shawl more tightly around herself. "That was the last time we spoke."

"You never shared a word with him since? Not at all?" I asked.

She shook her head. "As far as I know, we were never in the same building as one another since. I did all I could to make sure of it."

"Did he try to contact you at all?" I asked.

"No," she said. "Thank heavens."

"Hmm..." I said. "Well, it certainly seems clear that you do not think highly of him."

"Of course not," she said, her brow furrowing. "How could I, after the way he treated me?"

This certainly was motivation. Good, clear motivation.

There might not need to be any reason to look elsewhere.

"When did all this happen?" Eugene asked.

"Almost six months ago..." she said. "Far enough that most people have forgotten, yet close enough that someone might think I was somehow tied to his death... hence, your presence here tonight." She shook her head.

"I have not thought of him for some time before this morning when I heard the news, and it all came flooding back."

I looked over at Eugene, whose attention was fixed on her, absorbing the information.

"I can understand why you are here," she said. "And I see why you might think that I would have reason to kill him. I will be honest and say that I thought of it when he left me like he did, or at least that I simply wished he would drop dead. Despite that...I never could have actually done anything to harm him, or anyone for that matter. They were the thoughts that anyone might have had, having been hurt as I was."

"Of course, of course..." I said, nodding agreeably. *I never once wished anything of the sort for Thomas. Is this just a confession of emotion, not murder?*

"What of anyone else that might have had it out for him?" Eugene asked. "Can you think of anyone he might have feuded with? Or had a difficult relationship with?"

"I really knew very little about his life," she said. "I knew all about him, of course. His accomplishments, his success...he had no trouble discussing all of *that*. But about anything outside of it? No, I cannot tell you. I'm sorry."

I frowned. That certainly seemed awfully convenient...

"Well...I think we have troubled you long enough," Eugene said.

"Wait, I think I have more – " I started.

Eugene laced his arm underneath mine, and steered me toward the door. "Thank you for your time, Miss Bellingham. Your information has been quite helpful."

"Certainly," she said, and followed us to the door.

She peered out into the hall after us.

"Should I be concerned? For my safety?" she called after us.

"I think you'll be just fine," I said. "As far as I know, the police have no interest in his death. Only members of the family wanted to find out what they could."

"Thank you again, Miss Bellingham," Eugene said.

We made our way back through the club and out into the street.

"I must admit, I am struggling with something," I said as we started toward the car. "I cannot decide if our Miss Bellingham is a fantastic actress, or is telling us the truth."

"I see no reason for her to lie," Eugene said. "Most of what she said could be verified by others. Your cousin said they had a miserable separation, and she confirmed it."

"Which is why I think she must have good reason to kill him," I said. "When she talked of him, the hatred in her eyes...it was as clear as crystal."

"I saw it too...but it wasn't directed at him," Eugene said. "Not really. It was at herself."

"Herself?" I asked. "Why?"

"He was just being himself. She knows this now. And while he treated her poorly, she is upset with herself for falling for his tricks, all of which must be plain as day to her now. Retrospect always gives us the benefit of seeing the truth more clearly. She is frustrated that she allowed herself to ignore what her eyes and ears were telling her."

"Well, I certainly know what that's like, I suppose," I mumbled.

"I realize it's disappointing, but I do not think she is our killer," he said.

"You may be right, but I'm not ready to cross her off my suspect list just yet," I said. "Even if it is a short list...I wish she had some further suspects to pursue."

"Yes, it is unfortunate that she knew so little of him. I suppose he was clever as well as horrendous. One of the worst combinations," Eugene said.

"Too true," I said. "If he went through women like water, then I don't think we will be able to go through them all. And if they all have similar stories to what Miss Bellingham shared with us..."

"Which is highly likely," he said. "From the way she made it sound, she later learned that he had been seeing other women on the side."

"Or maybe she was the woman he was seeing on the side..." I said.

"Right," Eugene agreed. "He was a barrister, yes?"

"Yes," I said. "That's what we've been told. Why?"

"Well...if his romances all run in the same fruitless direction, then perhaps the next best avenue to pursue would be those he worked with. He would have spent a great deal of time with them, and working with the law is sure to have its difficulties."

"That it does," I said. "I have a cousin who – never mind, it is not important right now. Yes, that would be the next best step, I think."

We reached the car, and he pulled open the door for me. I slid in, and he took the seat beside me.

"You were a great help to me," I said, smiling at him as we took off down the street. "Thank you very much for being willing to accompany me."

"I must admit I enjoyed myself," he said, grinning. "It was certainly a bit unorthodox, but the music was good, and Miss Crawford, you are quite the dancer."

"I have certainly had worse dance partners, myself," I said.

We shared a small laugh.

"Well, what would you say to accompanying me for some more of the investigation?" I asked. "I realize you must have a great deal else that you wish to do, but – "

"I would be happy to," he said. "I'm honored that you asked again. I thought perhaps my humming along to the music would have made you regret asking me to come along in the first place."

"Nothing of the sort, Mr. Osbourn," I said. "Nothing of the sort."

9

"So, where are we headed?" Eugene asked.

The next morning had dawned bright and clear, with the trilling of birds and brilliantly white, puffy clouds as tall as mountains. It was the sort of day that I would have much preferred to spend enjoying a good, strong coffee out on the terrace, but I was instead on the way to the next part of my investigation.

"Mrs. Burke's home," I said. "She left me her address and said that if I ever had any further questions, to find her there. Apparently, the funeral is to be there, and so, I feel it will be the place with the best chance of finding her."

"And she is Mr. Culpepper's sister, yes?" Eugene asked.

"Correct," I said.

I stared out the window at the passing countryside. I was beginning to dislike spending a great deal of my days in a motorcar, but it was the way that it was for now.

We must make of it what we will.

I shook my head, frowning at my faint reflection in the window.

Felix and I had said nothing to each other since the day before. I'd left the estate, gone to London with Eugene, and come home to a dark house. I rose early as well, and only saw my brother for a brief moment in passing after breakfast; he on his way there, and me on my way out. He gave me a quick glance, his expression entirely blank, and continued on. I might as well have been the wall, he showed so little interest.

My first instinct had been to tell him everything. But the desire quickly fled when I remembered how upset he'd been with me that I had taken on the job in the first place. He wouldn't have wanted to hear anything, and I knew that he would simply question my desire to continue on with it when I had found absolutely nothing useful.

I still wasn't entirely sure that I agreed with Eugene that Miss Bellingham was innocent, but for the moment, I found it better to trust his instincts than to question. Besides, visiting Mrs. Burke might give me the chance to ask about the club singer, specifically.

That was, if she remembered her, or even knew of their romance in the first place.

"I want to speak with Mrs. Burke again because when Felix and I were there the last time, discussions of the funeral cut our conversation short," I said. "My hope is that she will be able to give me names of people to speak with. I can't imagine she wouldn't have some."

"Right," Eugene said.

The estate where Mrs. Burke lived had more charm

than that of her parents. It sat outside the city, but was tucked away from the road, hidden amongst a thick grove of trees. The sunlight flickered through the branches, sparkling as we drove up the long, winding drive.

The grove opened up to a low hill and a pasture in the distance filled with golden wheat. "It's lovely, isn't it?" Eugene asked. "Reminds me of my brother's home back in Pennsylvania."

"Pennsylvania?" I asked. "I didn't know you had a brother."

He looked at me. "Oh...yes, I do. We haven't seen each other in some time. He travels a great deal, you see."

"That sounds interesting," I said. "What does he do?"

Eugene smiled. "He's a bard, believe it or not."

"A bard?" I asked, laughing. "My word, they still exist?"

"Oh, yes," Eugene said. "Trained classically, as well. His desire is to be as authentic to a medieval bard as possible."

"That's impressive," I said. "Is there any money in that sort of trade?"

"You would be surprised how many people love to hear him perform," Eugene said. "I have traveled with him more than once, and played along with him as he recited grand poems, limericks, and epics. He has no less than fifty different sonnets memorized."

My brows rose as the car pulled to a stop. "You come from quite a musical family," I said.

"Yes, you would think..." Eugene said, and his face fell. "I think it was the best way we knew to be able to share our stories with others...the good and the bad."

My stomach twisted. "The bad? What sort – "

The door to the car opened, and the chauffeur beamed in at me. "Here we are, Miss. Are you ready?"

"As ready as I can be, Ronald, thank you," I said through tight lips as he helped me out of the car.

I looked sidelong at Eugene as he stepped out.

What was all that about his story? The good and the bad?

I stepped up toward the house, my mind on Eugene's last words. He did not strike me as the elusive type, yet his cryptic description left me with many questions. Had he wanted me to ask? Had he meant to say anything at all?

I had not known him long, but he always seemed open. I found it refreshing after so many years of people so steeped in their own rumors and lies that it became difficult to wade through to the truth. He had not been like that. If anything, I found him terribly easy to read...at least, that was what I thought at first. Now, I realized he was simply that way with everyone. Kind, thoughtful, and generous.

As I approached the front door, I realized that was why his comment struck me as so...odd. It was clear he wanted to hide his past...but why?

"Shall I?" he asked beside me, smiling casually.

"Go right ahead," I said.

He lifted his hand and gave the door a knock.

We were greeted by a housekeeper, which surprised us. "Please tell me you are here with the music."

Eugene let out a small chuckle beside me. "I didn't realize I was expected," he said.

"Well then, hurry and come in," she said, sweeping us in over the doormat as if we were a pair of stubborn housecats. "I apologize that I am the one to greet you, but it is utter mayhem in this house today, and I won't have anything else out of order!"

I opened my mouth to retort when she gave us both a good push down the warmly lit hall.

"Go on," she said. "Last door on the left. You'll find Mrs. Burke there, she'll give you direction."

I gaped up at Eugene, who just shrugged as the housekeeper scurried off through another door, muttering under her breath.

"At least we gained entrance," Eugene said.

I sighed, shaking my head. "Come on, then, let's go."

The last door on the left opened up to an astoundingly large observatory, with an all-glass ceiling that stretched the full length of the space. It was much longer than most observatories I had ever seen, with a deep green carpet running the length and rows of chairs set up facing toward the opposite end, which rounded out at the very end, with views into the forest beyond.

I stopped short. "This looks as if it is set for a wedding," I said. I looked up at Eugene. "Surely, it cannot be – "

"Those were my thoughts, as well..." he said. "Which would be strange, given the circumstances..."

Tables had been set out toward the back of the room, each with incredibly intricate flower arrangements atop them, dressed in the finest of table linens.

It looked more like an elaborate dinner party than a funeral.

"It seems more like a celebration..." I said.

"Given his personality, I wonder if that is not the point," Eugene murmured.

Footsteps at the far end of the hall drew my eye, and I

looked to see Mrs. Burke leading a group of three or four into the observatory, talking to them over her shoulder. "...sure to leave room here for the ushers. And do not forget that I wanted four arrangements here, and here."

She wore her hair up in a twist atop her head again, today decorated with red flowers that reminded me of poinsettias that matched the ruby red of her dress. She pointed to either side of a square dais, situated in the center of the rounded part of the observatory, almost like an altar.

"Must be where the casket will be..." Eugene said, leaning in close to whisper to me.

His breath tickled my ear, and goosebumps bloomed down that side of my body.

I did my best to ignore it. Ever since our dance, his nearness became that much more...noticeable.

"Hopefully we aren't interrupting," I said, starting toward her.

"And another thing – " Mrs. Burke said with an elegant twirl around. She stopped short when she saw me, her eyes widening, lips parting in surprise. "Well, well, if it isn't Miss Crawford? I hope you have some good news for me?"

"I have news, though whether or not you see it as good, I will leave to you," I said. I glanced at the people surrounding her, recognizing them to likely be either members of her household staff, or hired help for the funeral preparations. "If you have a moment, we would like to speak with you."

Her green eyes, like bright summer leaves, leapt from me to Eugene, who stood just behind me. "Certainly," she said. With a turn and a wave, she said, "Go bring me those flowers. And Argus, do not forget to deliver my message to Henrietta."

The man she addressed nodded, and turned to follow after the others.

"Now..." she said. "What can I do for you?"

I looked around the room. "I assume this is where the funeral is to be held?" I asked.

"Indeed," she said. "My mother was so utterly beside herself with the thought of her beloved son's body being brought into her home that she could not bear it. My husband offered to have the service here, where we would be able to give him...a proper farewell."

She stared around the room, and from the small tug at the corner of her mouth, I could see she was pleased with herself. It was beautifully arranged, with ribbons tied to the pillars along the walls, greenery shaped into wreaths that hung in the windows, and potted lilies in each windowsill.

"I...appreciate your desire to honor your brother so thoroughly," Eugene said. "It seems life is blooming in this very room, with all the lovely decorations, and the grove of trees outside. It will be a fitting memorial to his life."

Mrs. Burke turned to him, her eyes narrowing. "Mr. Osbourn..." she said. "I confess I am surprised to see you with Miss Crawford, in lieu of her brother. I assume he had some other pressing matters to attend to?"

"He did, yes," I said, before Eugene could answer. "Mr. Osbourn has humbly agreed to help me. I hope this does not trouble you."

"Indeed, ma'am, it was my hope to help Miss Crawford as a means of showing my sympathies," he said.
"And to be perfectly honest...I find no joy in the fact that
it happened during one of my concerts. While it might
have been nothing more than coincidence, I will not sit
idly by while a killer gets away with such an atrocious
act."

"My...a knight in the making," Mrs. Burke said. "I am
appreciative of the help, Mr. Osbourn. You have my
thanks, as well as the thanks of the rest of my family.
Now, what is this news that you bring me?" she asked, her
eyes diverting back to me.

"We have looked into one of the women your brother
had been seeing, where the relationship had ended
poorly. We hoped to either find her guilty, or perhaps see
that she could point us to someone who was," I said.

"And?" Mrs. Burke asked, her eyes narrowing.

"It seems she was not the one who did it," I said.
"Thankfully, we were able to narrow our list."

She stared at me, her expression hardening. "Who
was this woman?" she asked.

"Her name is Virtue Bellingham," I said. "She is a
singer down at a jazz club in London."

Mrs. Burke shook her head, shrugging. "I do not even
recognize the name," she said. "I assume she was one of
the girls he was seeing on the side while courting
someone else in the open."

"That is the way she made it sound, as well," I said.

"Yes, my brother was well known for doing that..."
Mrs. Burke said. "Had the reputation of a scoundrel, but
for some reason, women continued to swarm to him like
flies to honey."

"We assume most of his relationships that ended poorly would have similar stories," I said. "Which is why I am not terribly keen to pursue any of them. If any do not stand out in your mind, then they most likely wouldn't have had enough reason to kill him. When we met, I had hoped to ask you more about his job, and those he worked with."

"Well, he worked for a large firm, and all things considered, he was well-liked there. At least, in the way that he brought in a great deal of money. My other brother would likely know more about all this, as I never cared a great deal for any of the work Edward did. I simply did not care. He could take the most outlandish of cases, but I knew it was all for attention, and as such, never gave him any of the attention he wanted when he tried to boast about his success. It nauseated me to hear about any of it."

"What of his colleagues?" Eugene asked. "Would he have called any of them friends?"

"I would hardly know," Mrs. Burke asked. "He never spoke of them, only his own cases."

"Would you happen to know who they were?" I asked. "I think my next step will be to go down to the firm and ask around."

"Don't bother," Mrs. Burke said with a wave.

"Why?" I asked.

She stared at me, appearing somewhat confused. "I thought that would be obvious," she said. "The funeral is tomorrow, after all. You are to be here. Many of them will be too, I'm sure. You can speak to them then."

"Oh," I said. "Of course."

"And it would give you a chance to speak with my

brother," she said. "He would be able to introduce you...if he isn't too busy arguing with my father."

"Very good. Tomorrow it is, then," I agreed.

As Eugene and I left the house, I was encouraged by the hope that I might finally be about to make some progress in uncovering the identity of our killer.

10

"I hate funerals..." I muttered, just loud enough for Eugene to hear. "They're always so depressing."

The observatory had filled, nearly every seat taken...but the overall atmosphere around us swelled with laughter, chipper conversation, and the *chink* of fine china. Meals filled the tables, cool lemonade filled the glasses. Everyone milled about, not a single person glancing toward the end of the room where the coffin, as black as ebony, stood in a solitary beam of sunlight.

"...Which is why I'm having a very hard time believing we are currently attending one," I continued. "Are we sure our driver didn't take a wrong turn this morning?"

"It is rather unnerving, isn't it?" Eugene asked with a low chuckle, though he did not smile. "Truly, the only person that seems to be grieving is poor Lady Culpepper."

I turned to see the woman, draped in black lace, hidden away behind one of the pillars nearest the casket, her shoulders shuddering as she cried into a dark hand-kerchief.

I rolled my eyes. "I have half a mind to believe that she is just pretending to be so upset," I said. "Given the way the rest of his family feels about him..."

"I would argue that his father seems quite grim," Eugene said, casually glancing around the room. "I don't believe I've seen him leave that spot beside his wife."

"Maybe you're right," I said, reluctant. "Well, then... where should we begin?"

"Finding the other Mr. Culpepper would probably be the best start," Eugene said, extending his elbow to me. "Let's look for Mrs. Burke. Maybe she can point us in the right direction."

We headed up along the outside of the rows of seats, my eyes sweeping the crowds. The reverend had already given his message, short and concise, at the request of the family. From what Mrs. Burke had told us the day before, they didn't want to lie to everyone and tell them all how wonderful of a person her brother was. It seemed harsh, but at least they were being honest.

"There she is," I said, spotting a group of people nearer to the front, standing in the middle aisle. Mrs. Burke laughed at something one of the women in the group had shared, and as we approached, the glances of the others around them gave her cause to turn and look as well.

"Ah, Miss Crawford, Mr. Osbourn. Thank you for – "

"Mr. Osbourn?" exclaimed the woman directly beside her, nearly twice her age. Her pale blue eyes widened, and she gazed in wonder at Eugene. "My heavens, is this *the* Mr. Osbourn? The pianist?"

"Indeed," Mrs. Burke said, straightening, a sly smile spreading across her face. "Yes, he is one of our personal guests today. Come now, Franklin, move out of the way. Mr. Osbourn and Miss Crawford, please do join us."

I stepped up with him, feeling pleased at my choice of asking him to help me. My relationship with him truly was proving to be more advantageous than I'd realized. Felix, while my own flesh and blood, had no reputation here in London, any more than I did. Eugene, however... His recognition could only help me.

"Mr. Osbourn, what an honor it is," said the woman, the wrinkles around her eyes appearing as she beamed at him. "My word, I never thought I would have the pleasure of meeting you face to face."

"The honor is mine, I assure you," Eugene said, smiling at her.

"What brings you to Mr. Culpepper's funeral, eh?" asked the man beside her, who must have been her husband. "Did you know him?"

"Ah...no," Eugene said, looking sidelong at me. "Unfortunately, Mr. Culpepper's death happened to be on the night of one of my concerts. It happened in that very theater, actually. I came to offer condolences to the family."

"A heart of gold," the old woman said, laying a hand over her heart. "How wonderful of you. How thoughtful."

"Well, don't take it too personally," said the older man, his forehead wrinkling. "Edward Culpepper's death was inevitable, reckless as he was. I might have suspected he'd have a short life. He never seemed to take any care of himself."

"No, he most certainly did not," Mrs. Burke said,

with raised eyebrows. She sighed. "Yes, Mr. Osbourn has been most kind to us. I considered asking him to play today, but I did not wish to associate his music with the morose malaise of death. He deserves better, of course."

"You are very kind, Mrs. Burke," Eugene said, tipping his head to her.

"Where are your siblings, Mrs. Burke?" I asked. "I have been looking for your brother and have not seen him."

"Ah, yes, of course," she said, and turned to point down at the end of the room. "He is entertaining some of our late brother's colleagues."

"They were among the first to offer their respects after the service," said the old woman, shaking her head. "It's quite sad, really."

"Yes...terribly sad," Mrs. Burke said, sipping her lemonade. "I cannot imagine why they would have wanted to get it over with so quickly."

"And who else is in attendance, Mrs. Burke?" Eugene asked, looking over the tops of the heads of their group. "There must be over a hundred people here today."

"Oh, undoubtedly there is," she said. "Family, extended family...colleagues, as I said. Friends of the family...most of the people have come to support us, of course. We have the very dearest of friends." She laid her hand on the shoulder of the woman beside her. "We would *not* be able to get through this tragedy without all of you."

I resisted the urge to roll my eyes. I enjoyed dramatization as much as she did, but it seemed excessive in this case.

"Is there anyone we should be introducing ourselves to?" Eugene asked.

He was right. That was a good way to ask the question. I had little to no idea if she or her siblings had told anyone else of their suspicion that Edward had been murdered, and maybe now was not the best time to ask.

"Well..." said Mrs. Burke, swinging around to look. "Might I suggest the man standing there near my mother? That is Mr. Fowley. He is a bookkeeper in town, as well as a renowned author. He would be very interested in meeting with you, Mr. Osbourn. Oh, and Miss Crawford, I think you would be most pleased to meet a one Lady Violet, who is a cousin of mine, and spent a long summer in New York a few years ago. You two might find a great deal to discuss."

These were meaningless names. True names of guests, no doubt, but these mentions were nothing more than to deter suspicion of my being here, and Eugene's questions about who to speak with.

Our goal was interviewing the barristers, the dead man's colleagues. People might wonder *why* exactly we wanted to speak with them in particular.

I smiled at her. *You are cleverer than I might have once given you credit for, Mrs. Burke.*

"Very well," I said. "We shall be on our way, then. Again, we are terribly sorry for your loss, Mrs. Burke. We do hope that you and your family will be comforted during this time."

"Thank you, dear," Mrs. Burke said, pulling her dark grey shawl more tightly around her shoulders, her expression quite sorrowful. "I am sure we will find the peace we are looking for."

That she most certainly would.

"Good afternoon, then," Eugene said, and together, he and I walked off.

"Who was that young woman with him?" asked the old woman, just as we started away from the group. "I didn't recognize her."

My blood boiled. I knew, somewhere in the back of my mind, that it was entirely unreasonable for her to know who I was. Coming to London, I knew it would be the chance I wanted to rewrite myself, to renew my reputation. But to have *no* social standing, no recognition –

"She is cousin to Mr. Richard Sansbury," Mrs. Burke said. "Come to do some study, I believe. And, if I am not mistaken, she is to marry Mr. Osbourn."

We were out of earshot before I heard the old woman's reply.

"Eugene," I hissed. "Did you – "

"Shh," he whispered. "It's all right. Yes, I heard."

My face flooded with color. "I hope you realize I have said nothing of the sort, and – "

"I am fully aware," he said. "It is only natural that people will talk, given how much time we have been spending together since the crossing from New York."

"I have never cared for the way some people just throw around those sorts of assumptions," I said. I realized the woman probably thought she was doing me a favor, boosting me in that way, but could she not have said something else? Anything else? Something that was true would have been better, wouldn't it?

Well, at least it would have them talking. That was sure to make its way around.

"I, for one, am pleased to be paired with such favorable company," Eugene murmured as we came to the back row of the chairs, and passed between some of the round tables on our way to the back room. "There are many others whom I have been hypothetically paired with, who were...less than desirable."

I smirked. "My, I do not know whether to thank you for the compliment, or scold you for the poor light you are shining on what must be many fine women."

"Some were lovely, in their way," he admitted. "But you are far superior."

My smile faded, and I studied him. "Why, Eugene...I almost believe you when you say that."

"It's true," he said. "You have all the social grace and charm that I myself have always struggled with. You are intelligent, sharp-minded, quick-witted, and have a breadth and depth that I have not often seen."

"Then you must not have spent a great deal of time away from your piano, Mr. Osbourn," I said, my heart starting to beat uncomfortably within my chest.

"Perhaps," he said. "Or you are simply startled that someone has taken the time to notice you, and you alone, and has not been turned away by what they saw."

I stopped, and turned to face him. "I have never been anything, if not myself," I said.

He gave me a wry smile. "Oh, I have no doubt that is what you believe. All the time I spent without my eyesight...it gave me perhaps one of the greatest insights to the truth about people."

"Oh? And what was that?" I asked. "Your sense of smell?"

He laughed. "No, my hearing. I could detect the slightest change in the tone of their voice. A small hitch, a sigh, a clearing of the throat. These are the sorts of things people do not notice when they are distracted by the expression on the face, or the body language. Without that clouding one's perceptions, it is much easier to detect the difference between a truth and a lie. It's really nothing more than a matter of intonation. And it is doable without knowing the person well, either, but it becomes easier and easier the better you do know them."

"And what does my voice reveal about me?" I asked.

"That you try to seem entirely indifferent, much like your brother, but you are doing all you can to stop yourself from feeling anything, even the good things. I assume it is because of something that happened when you were much younger, which would also explain your uncanny ability to look death straight in the eye and – "

"You are quite a keen observer," I said, somewhat shortly. "Though I am sorry to disappoint you and tell you that you are entirely wrong about me."

It annoyed me that the smile on his face only grew. "If you say so," he said. "All right, why don't we head into that back room, then? We have some gentlemen to speak with."

My face burned, and I looked away. "Of course," I said.

I started away from him, my insides writhing. Why did he have to say all that? Why did he think he knew so much about me? It was ridiculous that he thought I was hiding anything. And I was not at all like Felix in that way. I was not the indifferent one.

He wouldn't know it, though, would he? We have only known him for such a short time.

I reached the door, finding it open a crack. Peering in,

I saw a group of men standing around, some of them smoking cigars. They stood with Mr. Culpepper, the eldest brother of the family, who seemed in the middle of some very amusing story.

I pushed the door open, Eugene at my heels, and strolled inside.

The five men turned to look at me, one by one, and Mr. Culpepper smiled. "Miss Crawford, I am glad to see that you came today. My sister told me you might."

"Yes sir, I would not miss it," I said. "I assume these are the colleagues of the late Edward?"

"Indeed they are," Mr. Culpepper said, as he gestured to the other four. "These are three of the barristers in the law firm where my brother worked, Misters Blake, Quill, and Lawson, and his personal assistant and friend, Mr. Boulton."

"How do you do, gentlemen?" I asked, approaching the group.

"Ah, and who is this fine young lady?" asked the rotund, balding man who I thought to be the aforementioned Mr. Quill.

"This is Miss Crawford, a family friend, and Mr. Osbourn, a friend of hers."

How interesting that he introduced Mr. Osbourn as *my* friend.

"What brings such a pretty young lady into this room full of grumpy men?" asked Mr. Blake, a spindly man with thinning, dark hair and a long, narrow nose. "We would only depress you."

"I am sure you could never do that," I said, smiling politely.

"My sister was telling Miss Crawford about the cases

that Edward used to take on," Mr. Culpepper said. "She was curious about what it was like, working with him."

I gave him an appreciative smile. It seemed he knew precisely the reason I'd wandered back here.

"Oh, well, your brother was quite the interesting fellow, wasn't he?" Mr. Quill said. "He brought a great deal of prestige to our firm and drew many new clients to us. We were always appreciative of that."

"Yes, he will be forever missed," said Mr. Lawson, a quiet, withdrawn sort who averted his eyes as soon as I approached. I thought he likely never spoke with women.

"I am sorry, but I must interject," said Mr. Boulton, a man almost a head taller than the others with the build of a coat rack, and likely only a few years older than I. "Mr. Osbourn, sir? Are you the pianist?"

"Yes, I am," Eugene said.

Mr. Boulton nodded, his brow furrowing, and shot him a nervous smile. "I thought I recognized your name. It is – well, it is a surprise to see you here, of all places. Did you know the deceased?"

"Not personally, no, I never had the pleasure," Eugene said. "It is rather tragic, you see. I am sure you heard of his death taking place at a concert?"

"After the intermission, yes," Mr. Boulton said, his expression grim compared to those of his colleagues. "It didn't happen to be during your concert, did it?"

"Indeed, it was," Eugene said, sadly. "I only wish to be here to offer my condolences to the family. Of course, I would not wish what they are having to endure upon anyone, but I certainly regret that it occurred during one of my performances."

"It is not at all your fault, Mr. Osbourn," Mr. Culpepper said. "We don't blame you in the least."

"I know," Eugene said. "Nevertheless, I feel somewhat responsible."

"He had a heart condition," Mr. Boulton said. "It could have happened at any minute."

"Yes, I heard that as well," Mr. Quill said. "So unfortunate, for his family but also for his clients."

I looked over at Mr. Culpepper. Part of me wanted to ask if there was any sort of truth to the heart condition rumor, but he had just stepped away from the group, his head bent low, speaking to one of the servants.

"Yes, he is not the first barrister our firm has lost to death," said Mr. Blake. "But he is certainly the youngest."

"Yes...first funeral for someone younger than I," agreed Mr. Quill.

"It does seem sudden..." I said, some of my impatience leaking through. "His death, I mean."

Mr. Boulton looked at me when I spoke, his face paling. "It has unsettled us all," he said.

"You speak of the loss to his clients. What of him as a person?" I asked. "Surely you have some stories about him, on this day in which we are remembering his life and legacy?"

The four men turned and looked at one another.

"Well, Mr. Boulton...you and he were friends," Mr. Quill said generously, pointing his smoking cigar toward the younger man. "They went to law school together."

"Did you?" I asked, turning my attention to him.

"Yes, and the poor lad, smarter than Edward in every way, did not pass the bar exam while Edward did," chuckled Mr. Blake. "He studied for weeks while Edward spent the night before trying to soak up as much as he could."

Mr. Culpepper had returned. "Yes, it was one of Edward's most...*charming* characteristics, being able to just squeak by on things without all the effort."

Mr. Boulton tried to smile, but it turned quickly into a grimace as he looked away.

"Well, Mr. Boulton, perhaps you should consider taking the bar again, now that we have a position available at the firm," Mr. Quill said. "It would certainly be a step up from assisting the late Mr. Culpepper, yes?"

"Oh, yes...I suppose so," Mr. Boulton said.

An uncomfortable silence spread through the group, awkward and oddly timed.

"So you really all believe it was heart failure?" Eugene asked.

"What else could it have been?" Mr. Blake asked.

"Yes, dropping dead like he did," Mr. Quill said. "So tragic."

"Such a sad thing," said Mr. Lawson.

All the false sorrow made me ill, but I tried not to show how little I believed any of them.

"Pardon me for a moment, gentlemen..." Mr. Boulton said, turning away and heading toward the door.

I watched him go, my eyes following after him.

This man might be able to give us more of the information we are after.

"We should follow him..." I whispered to Eugene, turning to pretend I was glancing over my shoulder. "Speak to him more privately," I added.

"Right," Eugene murmured. He reached into the front pocket of his coat and pulled free his pocket watch. "Well, gentlemen, I do hate to leave so soon, but I must unfortunately make it to a rehearsal this evening. Mr. Culpepper..." he said, extending his hand. "My deepest condolences to you and your family. I hope you will all find peace during this time."

"Thank you, Mr. Osbourn and Miss Crawford," Mr. Culpepper said, taking Eugene's hand and shaking. He glanced at me. "And Miss Crawford, I trust that you have everything you need for that particular thing we have asked you to get?"

"I am certainly working on acquiring all the pieces," I said, dipping my head. "But do not worry. I believe I will have it delivered to you sooner than you think."

"Wonderful," he said. "Mrs. Burke will be quite pleased. As will my mother."

"I certainly hope so," I said.

Eugene and I made our way toward the door, and I heard Mr. Quill ask, "Now you have me intrigued, Mr. Culpepper, with all this secretive talk. What is it that you have tasked her with?"

"Oh, it's nothing really," he said. "Something that will help our family to memorialize our brother."

Memorialize...what an interesting way to think of it.

11

M r. Boulton was much quicker than I had expected, and did not make his way back out to the rest of the funeral attendees. Instead, he ducked from the observatory and out into the rest of the manor.

"I wonder where he is off to..." I murmured.

"Let's go and see," Eugene said.

We went out into the hall, the din of the voices and eating in the observatory fading into the background. The hush of the quiet house beyond pressed in against us, making my ears ring.

We didn't have to look long, as we found him pacing back and forth in front of the front doors, much to the dismay of the housekeeper, who swarmed around him like an angry hornet.

"I shouldn't have come," Mr. Boulton said, his palm flat against his forehead. "This was a mistake."

"Mr. Boulton, are you all right?" Eugene asked as we approached.

"He is inconsolable," the housekeeper said, her fists planted on her hips. "I just found him like this, he won't listen to a word I say!"

"Mr. Boulton," I said. "Mr. Boulton, would you stop a moment – "

"I shouldn't have come..." he murmured again, his gaze distant, glazed.

I stepped into his path. "Mr. Boulton!"

He stopped, just before he collided with me. He looked up, and seemed startled. "I'm – I'm sorry, am I in the way? I didn't mean to block the entrance. If you need to get by – "

"We want to talk to you," I said. "If you would give us a few moments of your time."

He looked around, eyeing Eugene and the house-keeper. "I...all right," I said. "What did you need?"

I looked over at the housekeeper. "Is there a room that we might use?"

The housekeeper nodded, and walked to the door nearest to her. "In here," she said. "Please, just calm him down. I do not wish to distress Mrs. Burke or the rest of the family."

"Of course," I said. "Mr. Boulton, would you come with us?"

Suspicious though he clearly was, he followed us into the small parlor off the front door.

The housekeeper mercifully closed the door behind us, and immediately, Mr. Boulton turned to us. "I really would like to just be alone," he said. "It would be best for me, best for everyone, if I were to go home now."

"We understand that you were one of Mr. Culpepper's friends," I said. "Is that true?"

Mr. Boulton rubbed his hands together, looking out the window. "I – Yes," he said. "We were friends."

"From what we have heard, he was not friendly with many," Eugene said. "He had a bit of a...brash personality."

"Brash? I – I don't know if I would say that," Mr. Boulton said, shaking his head. "Look, I really don't want to talk about him. About this."

His nervousness appeared genuine, but something about it seemed...off to me.

Eugene's words played again in my head.

I could detect the slightest change in the tone of their voice. A small hitch, a sigh, a clearing of the throat. These are the sorts of things that people do not notice when they are distracted by the expression on their face, or their body language.

It was enough to tell the difference between a truth and a lie.

"Mr. Boulton..." I said, in as gentle a tone as I could muster. "We understand this must be a very difficult day for you. Funerals are never easy for anyone, but especially for those who were close to the deceased. Our desire is not to stir up painful feelings. What we want is to try and – "

"Help me?" Mr. Boulton asked. "How?"

"By giving you a chance to talk," Eugene said. "Sometimes the very best thing for the pain is to work through it by talking."

"And what could you want me to talk about?" Mr. Boulton asked. "Have you ever considered that I do not want to talk about him? I never should have come to this funeral. I debated and debated about it...and before I knew it, I was here, sitting there...watching his casket...hearing everyone saying over and over again that he was...really gone."

"He would have been touched that you were here," Eugene said. "Though I am certain he wouldn't have wanted you to be so distraught."

Mr. Boulton shook his head. "I don't know if that's true..."

"Why do you think that?" I asked.

"It's...complicated," he said. "We used to be great friends, but he...he changed. I don't know if he would have been happy for me to be here. In fact...I am quite sure I am the last person he would have wanted at his funeral."

"This is perhaps one of the worst times to be so hard on yourself," I said. "All it is going to do is – "

"You don't understand," said Mr. Boulton, shaking his head. "We...we were close, once upon a time, but in the past few years our friendship has been...strained."

"Did you have a falling out?" Eugene asked.

"One might call it that," Mr. Boulton said. "We never had the chance to make amends...not that he or I would have actually – "

"What happened?" I asked. I was growing weary of dancing around questions about the late Mr. Culpepper. He was a scoundrel, a fool, and despised by almost everyone. Why did it seem like everyone wanted to simply avoid talking about him?

I wanted more direct answers, and I wanted them *now*.

Mr. Boulton sighed, turning to look for a seat behind

him. He found a wooden chair beside a writing desk and sat down.

Eugene and I did the same, in nearby armchairs.

"We were great friends, at one point..." he said. "We met in law school, the very first class we ever took. Ethics. He and I ended up sitting beside one another, and we both found the professor...well, insufferable. We hit it off and began to spend a great deal of time together. He was intelligent, certainly, but most of his skill came from his ability to charm everyone, including our professors."

"His sister said he was rather funny like that," I said.

"At first, I found it amusing," Mr. Boulton said. "He would show up to class without his work done, without the required reading complete, and he would somehow be able to talk his way out of it. It floored the rest of the class, but I was simply impressed. He had a way of speaking with people that I had never known. The strangest part is that they knew he was attempting to pull the wool over their eyes, but they listened to him all the same."

We've heard something similar from Miss Bellingham...

"We did everything together," Mr. Boulton said. "Everyone liked him, and therefore, liked me. So when he would ask to copy my notes or have me complete an assignment for him, I thought nothing of it. It was easy payment, you see, to be his friend."

I glanced sidelong at Eugene as Mr. Boulton dipped his head. Eugene's brow furrowed in question, too. Did he really believe Edward Culpepper thought of him as a friend and equal? He sounded like nothing more than a lackey to me.

"Whenever I needed someone to talk to, Edward was

there for me," Mr. Boulton went on. "We stood by each other, through thick and thin. We were always there to support one another."

"It is clear to me that you were a very good friend to him," Eugene said. "In what ways did he support you?"

Mr. Boulton blinked at him, his expression blank. "I've already said. He always wanted me at his side. Wherever he went, I went as well."

Like a dog.

"No one understood me the way he did," he said. "Which is why I always thought that...well, it doesn't matter now, does it? Those days are dead...and so is my friend."

He exhaled heavily, and got to his feet.

"My apologies," he said. "This is...this is all very difficult for me to deal with right now. I...I think I must be going."

"But, Mr. Boulton, there are some further – " I said, but Eugene reached out and laid his hand on my own, shaking his head.

I had half a mind to argue with him, but Mr. Boulton was already at the door, ducking out into the hall.

"Let him go..." Eugene said with a heavy sigh. "I don't think we were going to get much more out of him, anyway."

"Well, at least he seemed to be more of himself there, toward the end," I said.

"I think we might have done him a service, giving him the chance to speak," Eugene said. "It is clear Edward Culpepper's death has grieved him deeply."

"Yes, but something did not sit right with me," I said.

"I know precisely what you mean," Eugene said,

standing to his feet, brushing off the front of his suit. "That man was being used to further Culpepper's ends and didn't even realize it."

I frowned at Eugene, also getting up. "He did seem a bit like an eager, simple dog, didn't he?" I asked.

"It is obvious the only reason Culpepper kept him around was as a means of making himself look better to everyone else," Eugene said. "I imagine he ordered him around like his own personal servant."

"And you do not suppose Mr. Boulton was aware of that?" I asked.

Eugene shook his head, pursing his lips. "I highly doubt it," he said. "You heard the way he spoke of the man."

"I agree that he idolized his friend," I said. "I imagine that to Mr. Boulton, Mr. Culpepper was everything he wanted to be. He strikes me as the studious type, while Mr. Culpepper was the one who did everything he could to put as little effort in as possible. I can see how that might have made Mr. Boulton jealous."

"But instead of jealousy, Boulton simply hung onto everything he did and said," Eugene added. "Mr. Boulton may very well have been the sort to not have the most... graceful of social etiquettes. Culpepper was no doubt invited to places and events that Boulton would have only dreamed of attending. It was his own way to fame."

"I had not considered it like that," I said. "It was more than just affirmative attention."

Eugene nodded. "I really do believe he thinks that he and Mr. Culpepper were friends, but it was far more selfish than either of them might have admitted. Edward Culpepper needed a friend who would boast about and praise him, and Boulton needed a friend who would artificially help him to climb the social ladder."

"Interesting..." I said, but sighed. "It's annoying, though, that I cannot seem to find anyone with sufficient motivation to kill Mr. Culpepper, even as hated as he was."

Eugene shrugged. "If we have learned anything, Mr. Culpepper was the bewitching sort. Maybe we need to shift our thinking a little. Is there anyone we know that saw through his antics? Someone who was never fooled by them in the first place, not taken in by his alluring behavior?"

I folded my arms. "I imagine there must be someone," I said.

"Former friends and lovers, as much as they might have disliked him, still felt enough loyalty that they wouldn't harm him," Eugene said. "It has to be someone else."

"Obviously," I said. "But who?"

12

I couldn't sleep.

The pressure to find the killer kept me from the exhaustion that made my eyes itch and my muscles ache. Even as I lay stretched out in the plush, comfortable bed in the guest room that Richard had so kindly provided, I could not remain still. I thrashed about, the frustration and the annoyance at being entirely empty handed preventing my mind from settling. I found no peace.

All I did find were questions, bubbling up in my mind. Fear began to gnaw at my insides, and I began to wonder if the killer was someone entirely random, not familiar with Mr. Culpepper at all. If this was the work of a random lunatic who simply liked to kill whoever was convenient, than what hope did I have of finding such a person?

The police wanted nothing to do with the case, which also made me wonder whether or not there even was a case in the first place. Was the victim's family simply paranoid? Or reluctant to admit that he might have died of natural causes, despite his young age? Try as I might, I could not entirely figure out how his death could negatively impact them. Would a murder scandal really be a way in which they would want to draw attention to themselves?

Of course, it is. Some families back in New York would have done anything to get people talking about them.

When dawn finally rose, I realized there really was only one option for me.

I had to go see Mrs. Burke again.

It aggravated me, but what other choice did I have at this point? I could not simply will the answer into existence, and she was not being terribly forthcoming with names of people that I might interact with. All the directions she had pointed me in had come up dry. Was that her fault? Did she even know that she had done such a thing?

Likely not.

I rose before the sun and dressed myself in a pleated, shin-length lilac skirt, paired with a sheer voile blouse, embroidered around the collar and tied at the waist with a sash. A pair of heeled pumps, a ribbon-trimmed cloche hat, and a pearl necklace with matching bracelet completed the appearance I wanted to convey, one of casual elegance.

As the golden rays of the sun peeked up over the horizon, I sent a housemaid down to the motorcar garage to fetch the chauffeur, Ronald, who kept his personal quarters there.

It did not take him long to bring the car around, and soon we were on the way to the Burke estate.

We arrived just before nine, which I knew was rather uncouth. The funeral was over now, but even still, there were a great many cars remaining in the drive. They must have had many guests stay, perhaps family from other parts of the country.

Well, this might prove interesting...will she take the time to speak with me?

I had come this far, I needed to follow through.

I approached the door, and was greeted this time by the butler, an elderly man that I recognized from the day before, named...Clarkson, I believed?

"Ah, you are...Miss Crawley, yes?" he asked in a feeble voice.

"Crawford," I corrected. "And yes. Is Mrs. Burke at home?"

"She is," he said. "Though she has not come down yet for the – "

He was interrupted by another voice.

"Clarkson, what is – well...Miss Crawford. I am pleased to see you here."

Mrs. Burke began to descend the wide, sweeping staircase above. She wore a dress of plum today, and her face split into a smile.

"Mrs. Burke," I said. "I do apologize for coming at such an early hour, but I – "

"I hope that you have brought me good news," she said, gracefully stepping down into the foyer. "I imagine you have. Otherwise, why would you be disturbing me the day after my dear brother's funeral?"

"Well, I did have some questions to ask you."

"About what?" she asked, her eyes narrowing. "Have

you or have you not discovered who it was that killed Edward?"

I stared at her. Did she really think I would have the answer already?

"You spent a great deal of time with my brother's associates yesterday, did you not?" she asked. "Theodore told me you went in to speak with them all, and were asking questions."

"I was, yes," I said. "Did he tell you I found the guilty party?"

"No, of course not," she said. "That is your job, after all."

"I have been narrowing down those who might have done it," I said. "As I said, I do not think it was that woman he had been seeing, but after speaking with his colleagues, it seemed as if they did not miss him at all. All they seemed to want him around for was what he brought to the firm."

"Well, of course," she said, planting her hands on her hips. "He brought them a great deal of money. It will be sorely missed, now that he is gone."

"But that is precisely what I mean," I said. "They would not have killed the man who was bringing in so much business to the firm. It wouldn't make any sense."

She rolled her eyes. "Well, aren't you brilliant?" she asked. "You have discovered who it is *not*, then?"

"I have questions," I snapped. "Have you ever considered that whoever killed your brother might not have had any connection to him? Or, that perhaps the police were correct and his death was nothing more than an accident, or the result of a health issue, just as so many have suspected?"

She glared at me. "So, you have come all this way to tell me that it was an anonymous stranger who killed my brother?" she asked. "Or that I have somehow made up his murder?"

"I am beginning to wonder that, yes," I said, my own voice as harsh as jagged metal. "You have sent me on this ridiculous errand to find the one person who might dislike your brother enough to kill him, somehow forgetting that the entire world had something against him, all the while giving me very little information to work with and very few people with whom I can speak!"

"That is *your job*," she snapped. "That is why I *hired* you!"

"I must tell you, madam, that your understanding of how private investigators work seems to be quite limited," I said. "I cannot simply procure lists of those closest to him out of thin air."

She stared down at me, arms now folded across her plum dress, her green eyes flashing like a rabid dog's. "You must not be terribly familiar with the profession, either, given your complete dependence upon me for everything." She sniffed, turning her head, lifting her chin. "I might as well have done all the work myself, for all the good you've done me."

My eyes narrowed and my fingernails dug into the flesh of my palms. "With such tact, I am perfectly certain you would have frightened those I have spoken with away."

She pursed her lips, nostrils flaring. "I employed you to find my brother's killer. It is not a terribly difficult request. I thought someone with your previous experience in tracking down murderers would be capable of finding whoever poisoned him."

"Which is why I have continued to come to you for clarification, for further direction," I said. "In order to find that person, I must have information to work with. I do not know your brother from Adam. The only person you have to blame for the lack of success in my search is yourself. Your limited information is what is resulting in these poor searches."

"I have no blame in this!" she exclaimed. "Get out of my house. Now! I will not be treated in this way."

Before I had a chance to respond, Clarkson had stepped between us and began to usher me toward the door.

Seething, I allowed myself to be guided back through the front door, and out to the car where Ronald stood, leaning against the door and reading a book. He snapped it closed as soon as I approached, tossing it through the open front window, before adjusting his hat.

Clearly, I had returned more quickly than he expected.

"I need you to take me to Mr. Osbourn's next," I snapped. "And promptly."

It wasn't until we were a few miles along the road that I realized precisely what I had allowed myself to ask in my anger. I might have been furious with everyone and everything, but why was it my default decision to go to Eugene? What did that say about me?

The annoyance continued to brew within me; annoyance directed at Mrs. Burke, at Felix, at everything that could have upset me within the past six months. By the time we reached the Osbourn family's estate, my anger had nearly boiled over. If I were a tea kettle, I would have been singing.

"Ah, Miss Crawford," the butler said at my arrival. "Another unexpected pleasure."

"Where is Mr. Osbourn?" I demanded. "It is very important that I see him."

"Of course, of course," the butler said, looking alarmed at my urgent tone.

He led me to Eugene, who had apparently settled in the study for a few hours of reading. He must have only just arrived, given the amount of tea still left in his steaming cup.

"Miss Crawford, sir, is here to see you," the butler said.

"Lillian," Eugene said, getting to his feet as I entered the room. "It is good to see – "

"Mrs. Burke is a hag," I spat out, and immediately felt a bit of the pressure release.

He blinked at me, the smile that had grown at my appearance falling somewhat slack. "I take it that something went wrong?" he asked.

I planted my hands on my hips, staring out the diamond-shaped panes in the window over the beautifully manicured gardens, and huffed. "I went over there to speak with her about the conversation we had with Mr. Culpepper's colleagues yesterday, and also to voice the opinion that it is possible whoever killed him had absolutely no connection to him, and she became entirely furious and sent me away!"

"Why is that?" he asked, stepping around the table to join me at the window.

I exhaled heavily, shaking my head in disbelief. "She

told me she thought that somehow, I should be able to do this entirely free of her help," I said. "It seems she thinks that I should be prophetic, omnipotent, something that is *not at all possible.*"

"I take it she is disappointed with the progress?" he asked.

"She may have very well just fired me," I said. "She cannot seem to understand that I have continued to go to her for clarification, for further explanations, because she has utterly refused to be helpful. She knows enough to tell me that a particular direction might be worth pursuing, such as his past lovers, or those he worked with, but any particulars, she is not forthcoming with."

He frowned. "Well, at the very least, you were able to narrow down those who did not kill him," he said.

"Yes…" I said. "I tried to explain as much to her, but she doesn't seem to understand that I cannot do this without something to go off of."

"I assume she was not helpful with supplying any more suspects?" he asked.

"No, not at all. If there was anyone else, she either does not know them, or I can safely assume that everyone hated her brother enough that any one of them could have done it," I said. "She did not care for the idea that it could have been a random killing. And she became especially upset when I said that it could have been a result of poor health. She did not even want to entertain the idea."

"She does seem very convinced it was that drink that killed him," he said. "And perhaps she is right."

"What if he was not the intended victim?" I asked. "What if the drink was meant for someone else, in the first place?"

"It is possible, of course," he said. "Though we have no reason to suspect that over him being the intended target."

"You're right…" I said. "I suppose I could track down the owner of the theater, find a list of all the tickets from that night, and contact each and every audience member to see who had a connection to the dead man…"

He shook his head. "That would be ridiculous, and would likely take you months," he said.

"Which would make Mrs. Burke even more upset," I said. "Perhaps that is where I should have started in the first place."

"It made sense that you wanted to speak with those who knew him," Eugene said.

I sighed, turning to look at him. "I hate to admit it aloud…but this case may just be too difficult to solve."

"And perhaps it will be," he said. "But even if you walk away from it, it does not change the fact that you have helped two other families, both my own and yours, in solving the murders that you have successfully figured out in the past."

I gave him a small smile. "Well…I suppose a little bit of encouragement is all right," I said.

"Why don't you stay for dinner?" he asked. "I realize it is still early in the day, but I could show you around the estate."

"That…would be very nice," I said. "I suppose I could do with some distraction."

"And we will not discuss the murder, nor the Culpepper family, nor even your brother for the whole night. Agreed?" he asked.

"Agreed," I said, my anger slowly fading away.

He did as he promised. He showed me around his uncle's estate, a fine place with beautiful gardens and a handsome stable.

We took tea on the terrace, walked through the gardens when the sun's golden beams stretched through the trees and elongated the shadows, and enjoyed a pleasant meal with two of his cousins.

"Now, this is a little family treat," he said after he and I had retired to the drawing room after dinner. He picked up a glass filled with what appeared to be thick, rich cream. "It's their version of ice cream, but they make it here in the kitchens."

"How is it any different?" I asked, taking the other of the pair of glasses that had been brought to us.

"You'll see," he said with a smile, dipping his spoon into the glass.

I took my own spoon, and sunk it down into what I had assumed would be thick custard, only to find something much lighter, airier, and almost pillowy. It had been topped with real cream, whipped and fluffy. I brought the spoonful to my mouth, and my eyes widened.

The treat, cold against my tongue, tasted sweet, with notes of –

"Honey?" I asked, looking over at him.

He nodded, taking another spoonful himself.

"And what is that other flavor?" I asked. "I cannot place it."

"Marshmallow," he said. "It is an old recipe, passed down by the family of the cook. The plant that is the namesake is difficult to work with, but the flavor is so much better when there is time taken to prepare it."

"I have never had anything quite like this," I said,

spinning the glass in my hand, examining the contents in the light of the fireplace.

"The cook is incredibly proud of the final product," Eugene said.

"As he should be," I said, going back for a second taste.

A few moments passed as we enjoyed our marshmallow ice cream. I might have licked the cup clean, if it were not for Eugene sitting beside me.

I stole a sidelong glance at him, watching as he scraped the bottom of his own cup, humming beneath his breath. He was happy, and it made me...content.

"You know, I should really thank you," I said.

"For the ice cream?" he asked. "Oh, it's no trouble. Unfortunately, I cannot give you the recipe, for I have been forbidden from knowing it as well."

"No, no," I said with a small laugh. I looked at him. "I cannot remember the last time I was so...relaxed."

His smile grew. "Well, that pleases me to hear, Lillian."

My heart hitched at the sound of his voice speaking my name.

"I can imagine that the past few months have been trying for you," he said. "I know you have been quite secretive about your past, and whatever it was that you left behind, but I believe I know you well enough to know that coming here was the best thing for you. Despite trying to escape whatever you have, you've been met with more difficulties with these deaths and murders. It cannot have been easy for you."

"It has not been the sort of life I expected to find for myself here, no," I said. "I had hoped for more parties and dinners and visits to the theater...and less crawling through windows in second stories to confront dangerous villains."

"I can understand," he said.

I continued, "And to be frank, I am surprised that you have been able to stand seeing me ever again after everything that occurred on the ship."

He shook his head. "I have thought about this a great deal, and the only conclusion I can come to is that you and I were meant to meet."

I arched an eyebrow at him. "That is a strange way to look at it."

"Not so," he said. "You coming into my life has...changed it, in so many ways."

"I cannot imagine your parents or the rest of your family would be glad to hear you say so," I said.

"On the contrary, I think my parents would embrace you, despite what happened on the crossing," he said. "We all realize my late sister's death and her recklessness harmed you, as well as many of those around her. My family regrets that, as do I."

"I do not know how I would even begin to feel if I were in your situation, and it was Felix who had..." I couldn't even bring myself to say it.

"I know," he said. "So do not put yourself through the mental torture of trying to imagine it. She was not my sister. Not any longer. She became a stranger to us all, exiling herself from us, and there was nothing we could do. Blood or not, she had to be stopped. We all know that."

I pursed my lips, looking away from him.

"However much I wish she didn't do what she did,

because of it all...I met you, and I cannot begin to regret that."

I stared at him.

"It seems...terribly strange, I know, to admit that," he said. "In a way, it sounds as if I would have wished for her death."

"I know that isn't what you are saying," I said.

"I do not know if we would have crossed paths, otherwise," he said. "I wish the circumstances were different, of course, but...here we are. It happened the way it did, and we cannot change it...but I am grateful that something good came out of the whole situation."

"Something good, huh?" I murmured.

He turned to look at me, and his eyes began to search my face. What for, I couldn't be certain. All I knew was that it made me feel suddenly vulnerable, and I had to look away.

"Lillian..." he said in a low voice. "I am glad, whatever the circumstances, that I was fated to cross your path."

I swallowed hard, turning my face to him.

My cheeks burned as his piercing gaze settled upon me once again. I could not look away.

He leaned a bit closer to me, and a strong, unspoken draw tugged at my heart, pulling me toward him, as well.

My mouth went dry, the palms of my hands grew slick with sweat.

The clock on the wall chimed, scaring me half out of my senses.

My whole body jumping, I sat up and looked toward the mantle, where an obnoxious gong sounded again and again to announce the eight o'clock hour.

Heart racing, I got to my feet. I stayed put, though, as

my legs felt as if they were made of the marshmallow ice cream and might give way beneath me. "I did not realize the hour," I said, brushing some of my ebony hair from my face. "...having such a nice time..."

Eugene cleared his throat, slowly getting to his own feet. "Nor had I," he said with a hollow laugh. "You will have to apologize to your cousin Richard for my keeping you so late."

"You must join us for dinner sometime soon," I said, as we headed together toward the hall.

"Of course," he said. "I would like nothing more."

He walked me all the way out to the car and bid me farewell.

It was not until I was halfway up the drive that I turned to look back, my heart in my throat...only to find him still standing there on the front steps of the manor, watching as I drove away.

13

"I'm sorry to bother you when I know you're trying to get work done, but I have some questions."

The next morning had arrived with pounding rain and rolling thunder. Lightning flashed through the narrow gaps in the drawn curtains, making the whole manor feel as if time had stopped somewhere in the middle of the night. Fires blazed in every fireplace, being stoked as diligently as they might be in the dead of winter.

Richard looked up from his paperwork and gave me a small smile. "I'm pleased to see you, Lillian. It has felt strange around here without you the past few days."

"Yes, I apologize for my scarcity," I said.

"No need," he said with a wave of his hand. He gathered up the pen and sheets of paper in front of him, stacking them neatly. "Please, have a seat."

I did as he asked, sitting as if I were one of his clients in the tufted armchair across from him.

He folded his hands, regarding me with a slight tilt of

his head. "While I realize you have been busy, I feel I must remind you your first lesson is to take place Tuesday of next week."

I blinked at him. "Lesson? What – "

It struck me, suddenly, and I furrowed my brow.

"Cousin, I am beginning to think that these...accomplishments, as you have begun to call them, are admirable pastimes certainly...but I am more than accomplished enough to find a husband."

Richard's eyebrow rose. "And you believe the only reason I wish for you to engage in these skills is to...find a husband?"

I nodded. "What other reason could there be?"

He sighed, sitting back in his seat. "The naivety of youth..." he said.

I glared. "I am not some fool that needs to be led along by a leash."

"And I have never once said as much," he said, still patient. "I am fully aware of your education and your connections. While painting, art, dancing, and horseback riding all might have their merits in helping young ladies to find a proper husband of standing, it is more about how they help to build one's character."

"I'm not following," I said, my eyes narrowing further.

He gave me a hard look, and the patience began to ebb away like chalk being brushed from a board. "I gave your brother classes to choose from, knowing that he had difficulties finding the motivation to stick to things. I gave you these similar options, knowing the sort of troubles you came out of. Why do you think that was?"

I folded my arms. "I have no idea, and I do not care to play games this morning."

"You were treated rather poorly, from what your mother has told me," he said in a gentler tone. "This Thomas Williams fellow who broke off your engagement handled the whole affair badly, and I know that does not even begin to scratch the surface." He added that last quickly, seeing the venomous look on my face. "But allow me a moment to challenge you. Allowing yourself to remain in your unhappiness, letting it fester, is only going to hurt you. Apart from that...in every relationship, there are two people. In almost every problem, both play a part."

I gaped. "If you are suggesting it is *my* fault that the – I did not end the engagement, he did! I did not go around town spreading negative gossip about him to everyone that would listen! I did not promise him one thing, only to turn around and do the precise opposite!"

"Lillian..." Richard said gently. "I realize you are still angry with him, and it seems that he deserves it...but have you taken the chance to truly look within yourself to see if there is something in you that needs to change?"

A guttural scoff came from my mouth, unbidden. "Of course, cousin. Why don't we take a look at it? You sound exactly like my mother."

He shrugged. "Perhaps I do. But you are avoiding my question."

I sank back against the chair, shaking my head. "I did not come down here to be lectured. I needed your help with something, but instead I am treated like a child – "

"Just one moment," Richard said. "I know you had questions. This needed to be dealt with first."

I glared at him, debating about getting out of my seat and walking out of the room entirely.

"I will say no more about Thomas Williams or your relationship," he said. "But I would challenge you to take some introspective time...because if you want any other relationship to work, there might be parts of you that need to change, which is why I suggested choosing from one of the pastimes that I did. They will allow you that time to think, to focus and reflect."

Not to find a husband, but to learn about myself.

I rejected the idea immediately. "I will honor my promise to you," I said. "But as soon as I have fulfilled your requirements, do not expect me to willingly continue. This is to repay my debt to you. Nothing more."

He nodded. "Very well. As your painting class with Gloria and Marie was canceled due to William's disappearance, it has been rescheduled for Tuesday."

"Fine," I said.

"Good," Richard said, meeting my resistance with a strong will of his own. "Now...What can I do for you? I assume that these questions you are bringing me have something to do with Mr. Culpepper?"

Anger permeated every thought, and I wanted nothing more than to snap at him for how foolish and simple he had made me feel. But I knew I had to do my best to keep it contained, at least for the time being, while I spoke with him about the case. I needed help.

"I have many questions about Mr. Culpepper, but as I think through them, I keep running into the same dead ends," I said. "He had many lovers, but all of them ended up despising them. In a way, it could be any one of them, but I know there is likely no way I could find them all, or interrogate them all. Most of his colleagues were entirely indifferent about his death, only seeming to care about the money he brought to the firm, which makes me believe they would not have wanted him dead, regardless of how unsavory he was as a person. His assistant seemed to be the only one who cared about him, but he was nothing more than an idolizer himself who still has not realized that Mr. Culpepper only cared about how good his friend made him look."

Richard nodded. "You are saying there may be too many variables to find the person who actually committed the crime."

"Yes," I said. "I know he died at the theater, during the concert. His sister is utterly convinced it was the drink that was brought to him, but that could have been given by anyone. I suppose I could go to the theater and find a list of every ticket purchased, and then somehow match those tickets with the people that purchased them – "

"Unrealistic," Richard said. "It would be impossible."

"Exactly," I said. "Mrs. Burke has not at all been helpful. When I have gone to speak with her, she thinks I should have been able to figure it out already, though she knows the troubles I am up against. When I ask for help, she gives me none, or very little. Which is why..." My eyes narrowed. "I would like to know more about her."

Richard regarded me with a look of confusion. "Are you suggesting Mrs. Burke killed her brother?"

"She despises him, just like everyone else," I said. "She was at the concert with him, the only person I can place beside him for certain at the time of his death."

Richard shook his head. "You need to be careful, Lillian," he said. "That woman has a remarkable reputation in the city. She has more connections than some members of the royal family."

"A lot of good those connections have done her," I said with a disgruntled raise of my hands. "I went to speak to her yesterday, and she chased me off for even suggesting that it might have been a random act of violence or that his death might have been of natural causes."

Richard's eyes widened. "Well, let us hope you did not vex her too much."

"Why?" I asked, annoyance striking me with its foul sting.

"She will find a way to ruin what little reputation you've built here," he said. "She will make up some nonsense story and spread it around as quickly as she can."

A chill swept through me, making my insides constrict. *It will be New York all over again.* "This is why I am beginning to think she might have been the one responsible," I said.

Richard shook his head. "No," he said, flatly. "It wasn't her."

I glared at him. "Why? It would make sense! It would be the best way to divert suspicion, being right at the center of everything. Hiding in plain sight, right?"

Richard continued to shake his head. "I understand why you might think that, but it is not her."

"Why are you so insistent on that?" I asked. "How can you know for certain?"

"Lillian, if you knew the woman as I do, as half of London does, you would not have suggested it in the first place," he said, an edge to his words. "Think about it. It must be common knowledge by now that she has hired someone to investigate her brother's death, even if she has made it appear that she is trying to keep it secret. You should know better than anyone; people like her *thrive* on the stories told of them, good or bad. They wear it as a badge of honor when all eyes are upon them."

I swallowed hard, but bit back the retort brewing. "Yes, I suppose," I said reluctant, knowing he was likely correct.

"Do you really think that someone would hire you, knowing of your previous successes in solving crimes, if they were the one who murdered the victim?" Richard asked. "They would not even consider hiring you, if there was any slight chance that you might find the truth."

I shifted in my chair, confused by his words. He scolded me yet complimented me at the same time. I said, "You think she would have gone and found someone with less experience, someone doomed to fail, if she was merely trying to disguise the fact she had killed him?"

"Why bother hiring a sleuth at all?" Richard asked. "Everyone, as you know, attributed his death to a health condition, a poor heart. If she had killed him, she would have happily encouraged that idea, and gotten away with the whole affair without even a hint of suspicion against her."

I frowned. He was right, of course. Why had I not thought of that?

I was thinking about this at one o'clock in the morning, that's why.

"Even if she was foolish enough to hire you, which I do not think a killer would be, wouldn't she have planted evidence to more thoroughly divert suspicion?" Richard asked.

I sighed. "Yes, you are right," I said. "And there has been nothing like that."

"There you are, then," Richard said with a dismissive wave of his hand.

I got to my feet, shaking my head. "Then it seems I am back to the beginning," I said. "I have absolutely no idea who killed Edward Culpepper."

"And maybe you never will," Richard said. "Perhaps it would be best to just set this one aside, and move on."

I chewed on my tongue. "Perhaps it would be," I said.

I thanked him and headed out into the hall, my mind working.

Perhaps it would be best to set it aside...but I just don't think I can do that.

I will find who did this.

I only need to look a little harder.

14

I f it was not Miss Bellingham, and it was not Mrs. Burke...then who could it be?

I paced back and forth across my room, having departed from Richard's study. I knew full well that Mrs. Burke had all but relieved me of my duties, but that didn't mean I couldn't continue to look into the case on my own. Besides, I could not see her figuring out the murderer before *I* did, and then she would have to eat her words.

"And wouldn't that be glorious?" I muttered under my breath.

What that meant next for me, however, discouraged me.

I debated going to speak with Felix about the whole affair. He had been with me the night of the concert, after all. I wondered if he would remember anything that had happened that had not caught my attention.

But I shrugged the idea off quickly, knowing he had been quite firm in his decision about not wanting to be involved. That, and after the conversation we'd had before the concert –

I shook my head, dislodging the thoughts like swatting away a spider web. It was *not* the time to think on those matters. I had more pressing concerns.

The next step, I knew, would have to be going to the theater itself. I would likely have to go and speak with every usher who had been working the night of the concert, every server, perhaps even the owner to see what any of them knew.

"Perhaps that is the place I should have started..." I thought, nearly catching my toe on the end of the trunk at the end of my bed.

That thought troubled me even more, making me wonder if I had simply wasted all the time I had spent running around London. Maybe I could have had the whole thing solved by now.

Frustrated, I groaned.

I might be in for a long, arduous process...but I could not see any other choice.

The door to my bedroom slowly inched open, and the face of young William appeared around it, reminding me of an eager dog following its master like a shadow.

"Hello, William," I said, slowing my pacing.

"Hello, Lillian," he said. "Father said you are quite distressed. I thought I would come and see if you needed someone to talk to."

My heart warmed, and some of the tension faded. "Well...some company might be nice, I suppose," I said.

He straightened and pushed the door properly open, striding inside. He closed it behind himself, looking around. "This is one of my favorite rooms, you know," he said, clasping his hands behind his back.

"Is it?" I asked, crossing my arms.

He nodded. "Mhmm. It has the best view of the lake."

I glanced toward the window. "Well, I thought your room had a much better view than mine," I said. "You can see straight across the water from that side of the manor."

"Yes, but from here, you can see my favorite tree," he said, pointing.

I followed him to the sill and peered in the direction he showed me. It was rather difficult to make out through the rain. "Is it that one on the shore? With the two large branches?"

"Yes," he said. "Felix figured it out as soon as I told him about it, too. I guess it makes sense that you both would think the same way, since you're twins and all."

My cheeks burned. "Yes, well...sometimes we do tend to think alike."

He sat down on the windowsill and looked up at me. "Felix told me you two had an argument, and I haven't seen you together in some time. What happened?"

I scratched my cheek. "It's complicated, William. I don't think you would understand."

"That's what Father keeps telling me about the time I was kidnapped. I know there is something he is keeping from me," William said, peering up at me.

I sighed. "I am not keeping anything from you," I said, trying to derail the conversation as quickly as I could. "We have simply decided to do two different things right now."

"You mean with Mrs. Burke?" William asked.

I stared at him, my brows wrinkling. "You're a clever one," I said. "I suppose it runs in the family."

He shrugged, but a small, proud smile spread across his face.

"I wanted to help her, and Felix did not," I said. "That is all there is to it."

"And have you been able to help her?" William asked.

I hesitated. "I...not yet," I said. "At least, not how she wanted me to."

William nodded. "So she is disappointed?"

"Yes, very much so," I said.

"And you are upset with her, too?" he asked. "I can see it in your face, since you sort of look mad right now."

I rubbed my hands over my cheeks as if I could physically peel the expression off my face, and sighed. "Yes, I am angry at her," I said. "I have tried a great deal to help her, but she does not seem to understand that – " I stopped, and gave him a pointed look. "How much do you know about Mrs. Burke's situation?"

He shrugged again. "That she thinks someone killed her brother."

"Well, then...I guess I don't have to dance around the issue with you," I said, sinking down onto the trunk nearby, looking at him.

"You haven't found who did it yet?" he asked, picking at a loose string in the circular rug that he sat himself down upon.

The weight in my chest only grew heavier. "No..." I said, reluctantly. "It is difficult when there seems to be an immeasurable number of people who would have been all too happy to – " I stopped again, reminding myself that he was only a boy. "No, I haven't found them, yet."

"People didn't like him?" William asked.

"No," I said. "Not really. He wasn't a very nice person."

"Neither is Mrs. Burke," he said, crossing his legs beneath him, resting his elbows on his knees. "I suppose that runs in *their* family."

I smirked.

"Did he have any friends?" William asked.

"Not that I know of," I said. "Well, no, that's not entirely true. There is one person who thought Mr. Culpepper was his friend, but I don't think Mr. Culpepper had the same idea."

"I know those sorts of people," William said. "I know a Rodney Wilkes, who is nothing more than a buffoon, but Henry and Franklin see nothing wrong with following after him like puppies."

"It sounds like you know precisely what I mean," I said.

"Rodney could not care less about the two of them, but because he lets them tag along with him whenever he does anything or goes anywhere, they think he is the best." William shook his head. "He doesn't even let them do anything, or let them play with his toys."

"Tragic," I said, my mind beginning to wander.

"It is," William insisted. "At least Rodney has some real friends, though, even if I don't like them much, either. Mr. Culpepper must have been quite terrible to only have one friend."

"Yes, I suppose so," I said. "I think Mr. Culpepper *thought* he had friends, but no one thought of him that way. He was...too proud. Too uncaring about everyone else. He only thought of himself, it seems, and it didn't matter what pain his actions caused others."

The words echoed in my mind for a moment, and I thought of Felix, and my actions. Had I hurt him? Had I hurt my parents?

Richard had asked me to look at myself, at my actions. Was that where these thoughts came from?

"His only friend must be very sad," William said. "I wonder if Mr. Culpepper was *his* only friend, too."

"He was a bit of a strange fellow, so it is possible..." I said. "Apparently they had been friends for years, did everything together. Their paths only diverged when Mr. Culpepper passed the bar exam, while Mr. Boulton failed and became Mr. Culpepper's assistant. At least that is what the other partners at the firm made it sound like."

I stopped, rolling the words around again in my head.

"In fact, they made a joke about it, didn't they?" I said, speaking more to myself than to the boy. I scratched the side of my cheek, thinking. "Perhaps I should have paid better attention to what exactly that remark was..."

"Well, that must not have made Mr. Boulton feel all too well," William said. "For him to fail the exam and his best friend to pass it. Mr. Culpepper would then have the job his friend wanted, and I'm sure that would make him unhappy."

"Unhappy, huh?" I repeated, mulling it over. It would make anyone incredibly unhappy, wouldn't it? Even bitter, perhaps.

I tried as hard as I could to think back to that night, to the way the partners spoke of Mr. Boulton and Mr. Culpepper.

"They mentioned that Mr. Boulton was smarter than Mr. Culpepper, very much so," I said, beginning my pacing back and forth once more. "They said Mr. Boulton studied a great deal for his test, and Mr. Culpepper hardly studied at all. That is not a surprise, given Mr. Boulton's later story about giving Mr. Culpepper every opportunity to copy his work and cheat..."

"I imagine Mr. Boulton was quite jealous, then," William said, lying back on his hands. He tilted his head, peering at me with keen eyes. "Wouldn't you be?"

"Yes...I imagine I most certainly would be," I said. "Mr. Boulton seemed to be all right with their arrangement, as long as it was benefitting him...but then, when it wasn't..."

My mind began to race, and my heart palpitated in my chest.

"I wonder...if he was not just trying terribly hard to pretend he was upset, when in fact, he was angry," I said. "He did say that he and Mr. Culpepper had something of a falling out."

"That makes sense, doesn't it? If his friend passed the exam without trying, it would most definitely cause problems between them, wouldn't it?" William asked.

"Yes, I think it would," I said. "But are those problems enough for him to murder Mr. Culpepper? I just don't know."

William shrugged. "Well...if he finally grew tired of being pushed around, maybe he would be angry enough to do something like that."

"It does make one wonder..." I said. "He certainly seemed nervous to see Eugene Osbourn at the funeral, as it was his concert where Mr. Culpepper died. Mr. Boulton interrupted our entire conversation to check and see why, precisely, Eugene was attending the funeral. Maybe I misunderstood his nervousness."

"Well, if he did kill Mr. Culpepper, then of course he would be nervous to see Mr. Osbourn. Maybe he thought you both had caught him," William said.

"Maybe," I agreed. "And he was the one to mention that Mr. Culpepper had a heart condition. He mentioned it quite pointedly...almost as if trying to deter any doubt."

"That is what he would want everyone to think," William said. "Maybe he is the one that started the rumor in the first place."

I looked at him, my eyes narrowing. "William, you are a clever, clever boy. I should hire you as my assistant."

William beamed at me. "Don't tell my father. He would never allow it."

15

I t wasn't until I was halfway to London that it really struck me that I had spent the better part of an hour discussing a murder with a ten-year-old. I didn't know if that would win me any favors with the boy's father, but I made a note in my mind to find something extra special for William the next time I went shopping. Something very special indeed, if he had helped lead me to the killer.

I managed to get the correct address from Richard for the law firm where Mr. Culpepper had worked. That had not been as difficult as I might have thought it would be, which gave me great relief. Ronald was once again driving me in Richard's car, and soon I was happily on my way back to the heart of London.

I had debated asking for help, but had only lingered outside of Felix's door for a moment. I knew he wouldn't agree to go, and as strange as it felt, I wandered away without saying a word to him. It was then, as I had made my way down the stairs, that I realized this was one of the longest stretches I had gone without speaking to my brother.

It unsettled me.

I had considered asking Eugene for help, but I found myself nervous about even being in his presence. The arguably wonderful day we had together had left me... confused. What frustrated me even more was that absolutely nothing had gone wrong. In fact, it was the best day I'd had in a long, long time. But the feelings it drew up within me were foreign and loud, and I knew it would be much easier just to do what I could to keep them at bay for the time being.

I had more important matters to attend to.

The law firm stood in a tall, brick fortress of a building on the corner of a busy street in the heart of the city. The river, which I could smell on the wind, resided to the south, and one of the wealthiest neighborhoods around Hyde Park a little to the east. A prime place for those in the business of taking money from those with problems that needed fixing.

"How long should I expect you to be, Miss?" Ronald asked as he pulled open the door for me, allowing me the chance to step fully out into the overcast day.

"No more than half an hour," I said. "If I have been longer than that, please come in and fetch me."

Ronald nodded. "All right, I shall indeed."

"Thank you," I said, and started up the stone steps to the front doors.

The entrance to the law firm might have rivaled the finance building in which my father worked, but it was smaller and a bit dated in comparison. Tall windows flanked the walls, draped in curtains of rich blue. Chairs were grouped together along one side, while a trio of handsome receptionist desks sat along the back wall, their occupants attending to other clients who had come in before me. A light fixture hung above me, large and wrapped in circular tubes of silver, creating an interesting cone effect in an attempt to modernize the space.

Feeling more comfortable in a place like this, I strolled over to the nearest desk, where there was only one person who stood, being attended to. I gazed around, my mind working through the plan one more time, before the receptionist called me forward.

"Good afternoon, and welcome to the offices of Blake, Quill, and Lawson," she said in a dry, croaky voice. "Formerly the office of Culpepper, as well, so I do apologize if you were here to see him... He's deceased."

I blinked at her. She reminded me of a giraffe, with a long neck and equally long face. "My, what a sad happenstance," I said, with all the casualness I could muster. "How fortunate it is that I am not here to see him."

She raised an eyebrow. "You aren't from around here, are you?"

"No, no I am not," I said with a smile. "But I am a journalist at the Oxford Chronicle, have been for about six months now, and I have come to speak with the partners about exactly the situation you have just informed me of."

"About Mr. Culpepper?" she asked.

"Yes, ma'am," I said. "It must be devastating for them to lose a partner like this, and under such *mysterious* circumstances, wouldn't you say?"

"To be honest, I did not know him," she said. "They hired me only two weeks ago."

"Ah," I said. "Well, might I have the chance to go and speak with them? Mr. Blake would be preferable, of course, but I would be happy to speak to either of the others. Or even one of the late Mr. Culpepper's associates. Any of them would do, really."

She glanced sideways at one of the other receptionists, who was busy filing some paperwork for the client she was currently helping. Not receiving the guidance she wanted, she turned back to me. "As far as I know, the partners and their associates have gone out for a lunch meeting," she said.

"Are they expected to be back soon?" I asked.

"I don't think it will be long before they return," she said.

"I would be more than happy to wait," I said, beaming at her.

"I don't know if that would be wise..." she said.

"I promise I will be no trouble at all," I said. "I will be as quiet as a church mouse. No one will even know I am here."

She did not seem convinced.

I leaned a little closer. "Between you and me? I really must stay. You see, my editor...he is quite strict. He would be *utterly* disappointed if he gave me the afternoon, sacrificed all of that time I could be working, to come down here and speak with someone, only to see me return empty-handed. Surely you can understand that?"

"I respect your work ethic, but they are simply not here right now," she said.

"Why don't I just go wait outside their offices?" I asked, still keeping my voice low. "It will allow me the chance to prepare my questions so that I can take up as little of their time as possible. I know how *very* busy these men are."

"They certainly are..." the receptionist said.

"I will not be any trouble, I promise," I said.

She stared at me, her eyes narrowing. "You are quite persistent, you know."

"I am," I said. "I am a journalist, of course. I am trying to get the best story I can, and hopefully draw more interest to this law firm."

She nodded at that, her expression changing. "I... suppose that would be advantageous." She looked over at the other receptionists, both of whom were still busy with others. "Very well. I will give you the chance to speak with them. There is a small waiting area outside Mr. Blake's office on the third floor. You may wait there. Stay there, and only there."

"Of course," I said.

"All right," she said. "Now...let me show you the way."

THE WAITING area was in a small nook in the corner of the building, surrounded once again by windows, with a long row of doors in sight, each of which had a golden name written across the glass window set into them. I recognized each of the names, along with the door on the end, further along the hall, where Mr. Culpepper's name must have once been, but had been scraped off. Only the gold line that had once underlined the name remained.

The receptionist, who I learned was named Deborah, left me in the waiting room, though I could see clearly that she was debating the idea of staying to keep an eye on me.

"I realize you are new to your job," I said. "And that makes you worry in a situation like this, that you have not had to deal with. If you want, you are welcome to sit with me."

Deborah looked around, her eyes drifting to the clock. "I would, except I have a great deal I need to finish before I leave for the evening."

"All right," I said. "Then I certainly do not want to keep you from it, but if it would make you feel any better – "

"No," she said, shaking her head, turning away. "It's fine. I suppose these are the sorts of surprises I will need to figure out on my own, aren't they? I wouldn't want Mr. Blake to think me incapable."

"Oh, no, not at all," I said with a smile. "I will be sure to tell him how helpful you have been. Now...I suppose I shall just settle in with a book until they arrive." I gave my bag beside me a gentle pat.

"All right," Deborah said with a heavy breath. "If you need anything, I will be at my desk."

"Of course," I said. "Thank you again, for all your help."

She gave me a nervous smile, and left me alone.

My smile grew as she disappeared. I had chosen the perfect person to let me up here.

Now...where is Mr. Boulton's office?

I started down the hall, taking careful steps so as not to draw attention from anyone who was nearby, nor those on floors below. If they knew the partners and their

associates were not here, they would wonder why there
were noises coming from their offices.

It seemed the partners all had the best, biggest offices
at the far side of the floor, while the associates and the
clerks were housed on the other side of the staircase,
along the back of the building, with views of the brick
wall of the building behind them.

I didn't have to wander far before I found Mr. Boulton's office, the name scrawled across a plaque beside the
door.

Increasingly pleased with my success, I tried the
door...and grinned when I found it unlocked.

I pushed the door open and stepped into the dark
space. The room smelled of stale cigar smoke and old
books. Shelves lined the walls, each one packed tightly
with books of every shape, size, and color.

*Well, I guess the tale of Mr. Boulton being a bit of a book-
worm was correct...*

A quick glance at a few spines told me he preferred
academics and non-fiction to novels. I stumbled on an
entire shelf full of law books...no, tomes...nearest to his
desk.

Either bitterness or determination kept them that
close to his work on a daily basis.

I drifted to the desk, knowing it would be the most
likely place to find his more personal information. I had
no idea what I was even looking for, but there had to be
something here to implicate him as the killer.

I found myself quickly disappointed.

He kept an incredibly clean work space. His drawers,
all neatly arranged, seemed to contain only the sorts of

items he would need to complete letters, with extra paper, pen, and ink. I found stacks of files, all named and organized in alphabetical order, which I appreciated but found irritating at the moment. After a quick rifle through, I did not see anything with Culpepper's name on it, apart from the firm's name that had been stamped on each file.

I found a few pairs of scissors, some rulers, and some paper weights, but nothing of interest or note.

I sighed, slowly shutting the last of the six inspected drawers.

Nothing. I came with nothing, and found nothing.

I wandered back out into the hall, careful to keep quiet as I made my way back down to Mr. Culpepper's old office. Disappointment washed over me as I peeked inside, only to find a cleared desk, empty shelves, and bare windows. The life, whatever had once been there, had been entirely removed.

"Likely before he was cold in the ground..." I murmured, leaving the room.

I looked around Mr. Boulton's office once more, at all of the books, and wondered if they held any secrets for me. It would take me hours to pick up each one, to see if there were any secret compartments tucked between the covers. It wouldn't be possible, and I wouldn't even know where I would begin to look.

I hesitated, looking around.

Everything seemed...almost *too* clean.

To confirm my suspicions, I checked inside each of the other offices of the partners. Some were tidier than the others, but every one of them had some sort of clutter around; work that needed finishing, files to be gone through, books stacked in nearby chairs for easy reference. They were lived in, and currently in use.

Mr. Boulton's office seemed as if it had been recently and thoroughly cleaned.

I swept my hand over the shelves, and did not find a speck of dust. The windowsill, the same. However, when I ran my fingers over the top of the window frame, they came away filthy.

Pulling a handkerchief from my bag, I wiped my fingers off.

Now, why would he be so fastidious with every surface in sight, yet forget the top of the window? Perhaps he was a stickler for tidiness, and so kept his office much neater than the others. Yet, by all appearances, he had just moved into the office, which I knew not to be the case.

So why in the world did he come in here and clean it out so well?

I believed I knew the answer. Perhaps he did not plan to be here much longer. Perhaps he intended to retake the bar, now that a new position was left open within the firm.

"Maybe he forgot to clean underneath his desk, just like the top of the window..." I muttered to myself, getting down on my hands and knees to look. My eyes fell upon a briefcase tucked between the legs of the chair and the well of the desk behind the modesty panel.

I pulled the chair out, and retrieved the dark briefcase, which I had entirely missed in the shadows upon my first search.

I paused, listening hard. I had only been searching for about ten minutes, but each moment that passed could be counted by the thunderous beats of my heart that reverberated against my eardrums.

The briefcase of worn black leather with a tear in the top left corner was unfortunately locked upon my inspection. It was a simple number dial on the top, which moved easily as I rolled my fingers across it.

Passwords were a funny thing for people. Felix always used the same numbers for his, which was the precise time he was born; fifteen thirty-two. Often people would use number combinations that had significance to them, so as not to forget them.

I looked around the room, wondering what I might try.

Mr. Boulton had to have been in his mid to late twenties. I tried a few different years; 1900, 1899, 1898...but none of them worked. He wasn't married, as far as I knew, so that eliminated that possible year.

I turned to see a diploma hanging on the wall, with the year and date that it was presented to Mr. Boulton when he graduated law school.

I grinned, and tried the year.

1920.

It didn't work.

I frowned, and tried the date, instead.

Seven-four-two-zero.

Click.

I flipped open the top of the briefcase, and saw that Mr. Boulton was not at all the neat man that he tried to portray himself as. The inside had been shoved full with papers, receipts, unopened letters, ripped envelopes... anything and everything that must have crossed his desk in the past six months.

I let out a groan. This would need careful combing, and for a moment, I debated simply taking the briefcase all together. But that would be theft, and I imagined it would be all too easy for Deborah to put two and two together.

No, I would have to make do with the time that I had.

I pushed some of the papers around inside, and a shade of pale blue caught my eye. I pulled it out, and saw it was the other side of a receipt with a familiar logo on top. It was the same flame symbol of the theater that Eugene had played at...the same place where Mr. Culpepper had died.

My stomach twisted. Would he really have been foolish enough to leave it in here like this? When I turned it over, I found a handwritten note scrawled on the other side.

It was an ingredients list, but with very specific measurements. Most of it seemed like a standard recipe for mixing a whiskey-based beverage but there was one item, some sort of extract, that I had never heard of. Next to its name were scrawled the words "a few drops of the extract should suffice."

I frowned. What in the world could the mysterious extract be? And why was it sufficient?

A drink order from the theater...and Mrs. Burke was so utterly certain that he had been poisoned by the drink sent over to him by an anonymous admirer...

This had to be it. Whatever this unfamiliar extract was, it was likely the poison that killed him.

A few drops should suffice.

It made sense...but it also meant that Mr. Boulton was not working alone. He had likely given this order to one of the bartenders at the theater who had agreed to work with him – a friend, perhaps? – to make for him, taking the receipt back after. Fool, he should have disposed of it. I wondered if the accomplice would talk and then I would have proof...

"What – Miss Crawford!"

The receipt fell out of my hands, as I slowly looked up toward the door.

Mr. Boulton stood in the doorway, his coat draped over his arm, hat in his hand, a look of sheer shock on his face.

"What are you doing here?"

16

"Oh, well I – I was just – just looking for you, of course," I said, slowly trying to move in front of the briefcase. I needed to close it and push the chair in without him seeing...which would be nearly impossible to do, I knew. "I grew tired of waiting, and thought I would see if you had anything I could quickly write you a note with."

"You came into my office, without permission," Mr. Boulton said, his expression hardening as he walked toward his desk. "I heard that someone was here from some newspaper."

"Oh, that must have been someone else, surely," I said. "I have only just arrived. No one was here when I came up to leave you a note."

Mr. Boulton's eyes narrowed, coming ever closer.

I needed to hide the evidence.

As I moved in front of the chair, my hands behind my back, I bent myself into an apologetic curtsy while slowly lowering the top of the briefcase back down. It was a strange gesture to make under the circumstances but I could think of no other solution. "I am deeply sorry, Mr. Boulton," I said, trying to use a bright inflection so as to cover the sound of the *click* of the lock. "I only just heard the news, and I had to come at once."

His brow furrowed, and he threw his coat and hat into the seat of the chair on the far side of his desk. "What news?"

"About – well, the theater," I said. "And the bartender. What was his name..."

I glanced over in time to see his eyes flash, fear quickly replacing concern.

I snapped my fingers, realizing I was, indeed, on the right track. "Oh, goodness me, what was his name..." I stepped away from the chair, sweeping the receipt with a brush of my toe underneath the desk, so he would not see it, but I would know where it was.

Mr. Boulton's eyes darted to his desk chair as he rounded the side, and his gaze fell on his briefcase. "I...I don't know who you are talking about," he said, though the crack in his voice gave him away.

He picked up his briefcase, trying to do so as casually as if he had left it there himself. He checked the lock, and I saw his shoulders relax. Well, at least he didn't suspect me of opening it. That was good.

"I heard he was taken into custody," I said, lying through my teeth. The words burned in the back of my throat, making my mouth dry and my heart race, but they were necessary. I needed to frighten this little mouse out of hiding...and fear seemed to be the best way to guide him.

"Custody? For what?" he asked. "And what does this

have to do with me?"

"From what I heard, he was your friend," I said. "And I heard he was charged with murder...the murder of Edward Culpepper."

Mr. Boulton's eyes darted away, and he quickly picked up his briefcase and shoved it back underneath his desk. "Edward...murdered?" he asked. "That's – that's just ridiculous. He died of a heart condition."

"Yes, that seems to be what everyone has been saying about him," I said. "Though his family knew of no such health concerns, which does seem strange...doesn't it?"

Mr. Boulton swallowed hard, his jaw muscles clenching. Sweat began to bead along his hairline, and the color drained from his face.

I had him cornered like a rat...and all I needed to do was get him to admit he either knew the bartender I was referring to, or he was the one who killed Mr. Culpepper. I didn't think it was going to be terribly difficult to do.

I watched him as he fidgeted with the buttons of his sleeve, attempting to refasten one that must have come undone. His fingers fumbled once, twice, and then he cursed underneath his breath when he could not get it a third time. "Miss Crawford, I appreciate your concern, but I – I have no recollection of this person you speak of. I am quite certain I do not know anyone that works – where did you say?"

I blinked at him. "The theater where Mr. Culpepper died," I said. "You must forgive me that I cannot recall the man's name."

"Right..." Mr. Boulton said, his brow furrowing. "I do not know – I realize that I opened up to you and Mr. Osbourn at the funeral, and I am terribly sorry to have put so much of my own burden upon you. But truly, I am doing my best to put his – his passing behind me, and you are coming here to – to what, exactly?"

"I thought you would like to know that the person responsible had been caught," I said. "I thought it would bring you peace, Mr. Boulton."

"Peace..." he said, and laid his hands flat against the table.

I studied him, his eyes searching the wooden surface, as if it would give him the answers he sought.

"Miss Crawford..." he said in a low voice. "Would you be so kind as to close the door?"

He didn't look up when he asked, but something in his voice gave me pause.

Perhaps he is going to confess everything...

"All right," I said, and I did as he asked.

When I turned back around to face him, I found a small pistol clutched tightly in his hand, his finger dancing around the trigger...the barrel pointed directly at me.

A chill ran down my back, and I froze.

This was not what I had expected would happen.

"How did you find out about Michael?" he asked in a hushed tone.

"Michael? Is that his name?" I asked. "Well, thank you for clearing that up, Mr. Boulton. That will save me a great deal of time."

His eyes widened. He had realized that he had walked straight into my trap.

"Oh, don't despair," I said, folding my arms. "I already know that you and he were working together. I do not yet know if you were the one who came up with the drink that killed Mr. Culpepper, or if he was, but I am certain the police will be very interested in – "

"Oh, you won't be leaving here..." he said. He nudged his briefcase beneath his desk with his foot, likely shoving it further out of sight. "Michael won't talk, and neither will I. This knowledge is going to die with you."

"If you were going to kill me, you already would have," I said. That might not be true, as I didn't know him well enough to predict his actions, but I needed to stall him. I was at a severe disadvantage now, but I had managed to get out of this sort of situation before, so I knew I could do it again.

I brushed my hands across my thigh...and my stomach went cold.

I was not wearing the garter beneath my skirt, the one where I usually hid my knives. I had left the house without them, without even thinking.

Why had I not considered the fact that I was putting myself into a dangerous situation?

"You do realize that if you pull that trigger...everyone will hear it," I said. "There will be no hiding it. The sound will echo through the whole building. Even if you tried to make it look like an accident, people will know a gun went off in your office, and they will find me dead. Once the authorities look more closely at you, they will surely be able to pin the murder of Mr. Culpepper on you, as well."

The muscles in his neck tensed, and a vein bulged above his eyebrow.

"Besides...I am not the one you need to deal with," I said, trying my last advantage. "Killing me would solve nothing. Not a thing."

"Does someone else know?" he breathed.

I nodded. He didn't need to know that the other person was only a boy.

He cursed once again, turning away from me, running a hand through his hair.

"It would be much better for you to make a deal with me," I said. "Or make a deal with the police. Perhaps with a plea bargain, you would only have to serve so much time in – "

"In prison?" he asked with a hollow chuckle. "I wouldn't survive prison. I'm an academic. Those monsters would eat me alive..."

He lifted the gun to me again.

"You are going to be caught one way or another, at this point," I said, raising my hands in surrender. "Let me help you. I understand *why* you despised him as much as you did."

"Really?" he asked, his brow furrowing, his eyes becoming slits. "I doubt you do. How would you feel to realize that you were nothing more than a pawn for someone else's success? That once they achieved that success, they would leave you high and dry, not caring whether you – whether you lived or died. I was nothing more than a stepping stone, used for my intelligence so that Edward could have the job I always wanted. I watched him treat people like they were no better to him than a mongrel dog, and never said anything...not until he turned and treated me, who I thought to be his closest friend, the same way. He only cared about himself...and it took all this time for me to realize it."

"I am sorry he behaved toward you as he did," I said. "But was it really necessary to end his life?"

"He ended mine," he said, his voice rising. "The way he sapped me of all my strength and energy, leaving me with the residual amount of time to be able to study, and it cost me...it cost me everything."

"Did it?" I asked. "Could you not have gone and taken the bar exam again?"

"That isn't the point," he said, slamming his free hand against the desk. "He could not go on treating people that way. I tried to confront him, tried to talk to him, and he laughed in my face!" He grimaced. "He never cared about me. I was a fool...but so was he...and he had to go. For the good of not only myself, but the whole world. Every woman he ever seduced, every client he ever swindled – "

The door banged open behind me, and to my astonishment, Felix stepped into the room.

"Felix!" I exclaimed. "What are you – "

He said nothing, instead flicking his wrist outward. Something glinted, and whistled through the air, before striking Mr. Boulton in the shoulder.

Was that...his playing card knife that we bought at the street fair?

Felix grabbed me and pulled me to the floor just a moment before Mr. Boulton let out a terrible cry, and the deafening *bang!* of the gun going off echoed throughout the room.

Before I had even lifted my head, my ears ringing, Felix had left me and circled around the desk.

As I staggered to my feet, my head spinning, I found Felix snatching the gun off the floor where it had fallen, and Mr. Boulton screaming, holding his shoulder as crimson blood began to seep between his fingers.

17

"You know, I really should apologize to you."

The car bumped along on the road, through the countryside heading back to Cousin Richard's estate.

Mr. Boulton had been handcuffed and led away by a group of police officers for holding until he could be questioned. I could thank the efficient Deborah for their timely arrival, as the receptionist had hastened to telephone the authorities, at Felix's direction. The police informed me they would be in touch with Mrs. Burke, which pleased me. I knew it was only a matter of time before I received a special note in the mail from her about my success, most likely with a payment enclosed for my services.

No one had questioned why Mr. Boulton was injured when they found the pistol Felix and I explained had been used against me. I had quickly informed them that he was the one who had killed Mr. Culpepper, and snatched the receipt up from underneath the desk.

I did not know if anyone else had ever looked at me with such hatred as Boulton did, when he realized I had somehow gotten into his briefcase, found the receipt, and hidden it without his knowledge. I was confident that once the authorities matched the note with his handwriting, along with the testimony from the bartender at the theater, he would be shown guilty before the week was out.

I glanced over at Felix, who had broken a silence that had carried on for a quarter of an hour or more, now. "Well...you need not apologize for your timing, at least. That was rather impeccable."

He smirked, and I found it eased some of the tension in my heart. "No...for trying to deter you in the first place," he said.

I furrowed my brow. "Yes, that was certainly wrong of you," I said, sitting a bit straighter like a preening bird. "You should have trusted me."

"I should have, you're right," he said. "Because as soon as I told you not to do it, part of me couldn't stand the thought of not learning the truth and I found myself asking Richard what he'd heard, or speaking with some of the staff around the house about the people involved. One of the cook's helpers once worked for Mr. Theodore Culpepper, and so knew the late Edward."

"Oh?" I asked, arching a brow. "That would have been helpful information for me."

He shook his head. "Well, perhaps not. All I learned was that Edward Culpepper was quite insufferable, and somehow managed to make a fool of himself wherever he went. It seems you came to the same dead ends that I did."

"Indeed, I did," I said, somewhat reluctantly.

"I should have come to you and apologized sooner," he said. "But I found myself struggling to bridge that gap. Pride held my tongue."

My cheeks colored. "Yes, well...we can't all be perfect, can we?"

"To be honest, I thought the whole affair would fizzle out and just fade away," he said. "It seemed as if the list of those who hated Culpepper was as long as my arm, and you would never manage to get through them all. I thought you would give up, and I could simply tell you I was right all along...and we could move on with life."

I glowered at him. "You were looking forward to reminding me how you had told me that would happen?" I asked.

He nodded. "Yes, which is partly what I am apologizing for," he said. "It wasn't until I found William earlier today, and he said he had spoken with you and you seemed to have solved the crime, that I realized you might be in danger. I hurried to your room to see if he was right, and you had already gone."

He reached down onto the floor and picked up the garter I had converted into a holster for my knives, and passed it to me.

"I found this, and knew you would surely need my help."

I took it, my heart sinking. "Thank you," I said. "For coming to help me. I didn't know how I was going to get out of that situation. All I could think was to try and talk him down, try to get him to make a deal with me so I could at least escape with my life, and then of course turn him in... but the best I had managed to do was somewhat convince him that if he shot me, everyone else in the building would hear it, and he would end up in prison anyway."

Felix shrugged. "Not terrible logic," he said. "Did it work?"

"Almost," I said. "And I suppose I should apologize as well. For being as bitter toward you as I was. I...allowed my frustrations to cloud my judgment, and knowing full well that we should have just sat down like the adults we are and talked everything over, I still chose to act like a child. For that, I am sorry."

He grinned. "Look at you. My baby sister is growing."

I gave him a shove. "You have no right to call me baby sister. Ten minutes older does not make you my elder."

He laughed.

I smiled, in spite of the event we had just endured. "Let us not go so long without speaking again...shall we?"

"Agreed," he said. "It felt wrong."

"Indeed it did," I said. "I was beginning to feel a bit strange, not having you to run things past."

"And I without you to keep me in check," he said. His smirk widened. "Though you had a chance to spend some time with Eugene Osbourn, didn't you?"

The pink in my cheeks deepened, and I looked away. "I needed help, that is all," I said. "And he was willing to help me investigate the case, when *you* were being so stubborn."

He chuckled. "Well, I must admit I'm not sorry you had the chance to work alongside him. I imagine he was quite honored. And...I heard from Richard that one of those days you were gone, you were not out investigating, but spending the day at Osbourn's family's estate? If I didn't know any better, I would say you must have enjoyed yourself?"

His words riled me, but I swallowed my anger, in favor of the truth. "I did enjoy myself," I said.

"Then have you changed your mind about him?" he asked.

"I am...beginning to," I said.

"Very good," Felix said with a grin.

The motorcar turned into the drive, and the weight in my heart began to ease slightly. It seemed as though maybe, just maybe, everything could go back to the way it was. Maybe those moments of weakness after William's return were nothing more than that; weakness. Felix often blamed himself for everything, and what he had spoken of our long-dead brother had likely been nothing more than that.

I needed to apologize for how I had treated him, based on that conversation. It had not been fair of me, and it had led to all of the difficulties I had endured.

"Well...I'm glad this is all behind me now," I said. "I shall be able to rest easy, knowing that I was able to figure out the Culpepper murder. Well, with William's help, believe it or not."

The chauffeur parked the car and climbed out just as Felix's jaw dropped. "William helped you solve the case?" he asked. He laughed. "What a clever boy."

"Precisely what I said," I replied. "I told him I should hire him as my assistant."

Felix gave me a sidelong look before stepping out of the car himself. "Let's not get too far ahead of ourselves..."

He helped me out, and the driver took the car back to the garage.

I reminded myself I should thank Ronald later for having guided Felix into the building earlier, when he had shown up outside the law offices, looking for me.

For now, though, there was something else on my mind.

"Felix..." I said, lingering near the bottom of the stairs.

The wind whipped around the side of the manor, ruffling my bobbed, black hair, swirling its short strands in front of my face.

"Yes?" he asked.

"I must clear the air, fully," I said. "That night, when we brought William home after the kidnapping..." I shook my head. "It has caused me so much consternation, but I cannot imagine that what I heard could be true. Not really, not in the way that you made it seem when we spoke."

His brow furrowed. "What are you talking about?"

My heart lightened slightly, but annoyance appeared. "I have spent all this time agonizing over it, and you cannot even remember?" I asked. I scoffed. "Perhaps I should not have said anything..."

I started up the stairs.

"Are you talking about...what I told you about Daniel?"

I stopped, nearly tripping on the next step. I turned, slowly, the wind nearly knocking me off balance. "So you do remember?" I asked.

His face fell, and he looked down. "I...do not know if this is the best time to discuss it..."

My stomach clenched. "Will there ever be a good

time?" I asked. "How could you reveal to me what you did, that his death, which I had assumed all along was an accident, somehow might not have been?" It amazed me just how quickly my mood had changed, how quickly the division had been reestablished between us.

He couldn't look at me. He slipped his hands into his trouser pockets, and shook his head.

"Felix, you always blame yourself for things that are not your fault," I said. "I imagine you have even blamed yourself for my decision to take on Mr. Culpepper's case alone, didn't you? Thinking it was something you did that pushed me away, when in truth it was my fault for pushing you away? I could have just as easily come to you and apologized, as I should have, and – "

"Lillian..." Felix said, his voice hollow.

It was as if I'd swallowed a stone. My limbs grew heavy, and everything else around me grew dim.

"I am not simply taking blame for his death..." he said. "I...I caused his death, Lillian. It was me. I...I killed him."

He finally raised his head and looked up at me.

Once upon a time, it would have been quite akin to looking in a mirror. Of course, his cheekbones were a bit more pronounced than my own, his features more masculine, but now...

It was as if I was staring at a complete stranger.

"No..." I muttered. "You are just trying to make sense of it. Felix, you wouldn't – "

He said nothing as he began to climb the stairs, one heavy footed step after the other.

"Felix?" I asked as he passed by, my voice shaking.

He still said nothing.

"Felix, you wouldn't! You couldn't!"

He barely glanced over his shoulder at me. "I did, Lillian..." he said. "I wish you would have just allowed the truth to remain in the past."

I stared after him as he went into the house, and then sank down onto the steps, my knees unable to hold my weight any longer.

It was true. I had been so hopeful, so certain, that it was nothing more than a misunderstanding.

Was this why Felix was so disturbed after the murder on the ship? I knew it had dredged up thoughts about Daniel's death for us both...but had it been more than that for Felix?

Was this why he didn't want me to pursue investigating murders any longer?

Did our parents know? Had he ever told anyone?

What am I going to do? What in the world am I going to do?

What *could* be done? Nothing would change what had happened.

Daniel was gone.

Felix had killed him.

What did that mean, then...for me?

~

Continue the mysterious adventures of Lillian Crawford with "Murder Behind the Closed Door: A Lillian Crawford Murder Mystery, Book 4."

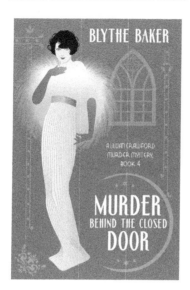

ABOUT THE AUTHOR

Blythe Baker is the lead writer behind several popular historical and paranormal mystery series. When Blythe isn't buried under clues, suspects, and motives, she's acting as chauffeur to her children and head groomer to her household of beloved pets. She enjoys walking her dogs, lounging in her backyard hammock, and fiddling with graphic design. She also likes binge-watching mystery shows on TV. To learn more about Blythe, visit her website and sign up for her newsletter at www.blythebaker.com

Made in the USA
Las Vegas, NV
01 July 2022